THE SEASON OF LOVE

In the far corner of the room stood a pine tree that reached just above Breck's height. About its branches were hung a number of adornments. Perfectly round oranges, bowed ribbons, and small brass keepsakes decorated the tree from top to bottom. Set among the branches were short candles of purest white, held in place by small sconces of polished brass.

Breck moved toward one corner of the room, the better to see Nerissa's profile as she continued to gaze at the tree, her brown eyes wide with wonder.

"Shall I light them for you?" he asked at last in a low voice that was just as mesmerizing as the tree itself.

He didn't wait for her to answer, but drew a taper from the candelabrum and began to light the candles on the tree. Nerissa clapped her hands together and watched him with a feeling of deepening anticipation. When he was done, he stepped back, allowing her a full view of the results.

The cand' l'ght amid the branches seemed to set the entire tree off the small brass tokens and bathe beauty.

Nerissa had been so dazzled. beautiful?" she asked ap ful thing I have ever seen

Nerissa felt a sudden and e wave of happiness sweep over her. She looked over at Breck and found his gray eyes upon her, his lips half smiling, and an oddly arrested expression on his face. . . .

Books by Nancy Lawrence

DELIGHTFUL DECEPTION

A SCANDALOUS SEASON

ONCE UPON A CHRISTMAS

Published by Zebra Books

ONCE UPON
A
CHRISTMAS

Nancy Lawrence

Zebra Books
Kensington Publishing Corp.

http://www.zebrabooks.com

ZEBRA BOOKS are published by

Kensington Publishing Corp.
850 Third Avenue
New York, NY 10022

First Printing: November, 1997
10 9 8 7 6 5 4 3 2 1

Printed in the United States of America

For Kevin

A hero in the making

Chapter 1

London, December 1816

Miss Nerissa Raleigh descended the front steps of the publishing offices at 18 Warwick Square with her manuscript tucked protectively in her arms and an expression of strong indignation on her face.

Her sister, Lady Anne Bridgewater, was waiting for her in the barouche at the curb of the crowded street, and saw in an instant that Nerissa's interview with Mr. Heble the Younger of Heble and Sons, Publishers, had not gone well.

"They didn't buy it!" said Nerissa in a voice of deep emotion as a groom assisted her across a rather treacherous puddle and into the carriage.

"Oh, dear!" said Anne in her soft, comforting voice. "And I was so sure Mr. Heble would think you just as talented a writer as I do!"

Nerissa settled in the comfortable carriage beside her sister with her manuscript clutched against her bosom. She cast a piteous look up at the windows of the publisher's offices as the groom draped a heavy carriage rug across her legs.

"I had such great hopes of having my book published, and I've worked so desperately hard on the story. Oh, Anne, *now* what am I to do?"

Anne gave the signal for her coachman to drive on into the crush of traffic, then patted her sister's hand consolingly. She peeked beneath the brim of the bonnet that covered Nerissa's shining black curls and was relieved to note there were no visible tears gathering in her brown eyes. "You mustn't be sad, dearest. *I* think it is a wonderful story that quite rivals any of the novels you and I have ever read! I think it is quite horrid of Mr. Heble to have thought otherwise! Tell me, dearest, was he cruel to you at all?"

"No, he wasn't cruel," allowed Nerissa. "He was quite charming, actually. He said he liked my story and thought it showed promise but it was in need of fixing."

Anne blinked twice and her eyes widened slightly. "Did he? And what else did he say?"

"He said he especially liked the villain in the story. He said I had quite a knack for creating evil genius."

"So Mr. Heble liked it after all! Rissa, you goose! You almost had me believing your story was rejected quite out of hand!"

"But it *was* rejected," Nerissa countered burningly.

Anne gave her sister's slender fingers an affectionate squeeze. "Goose!" she said again. "What else did he say about your book? Did he like the heroine, Lady Hester? And what of the hero, Count du Laney?"

"He liked Lady Hester very well, I dare say, for he said she was all a heroine should be. But, Anne, it's that dreadful Count du Laney that is the very reason Mr. Heble said he would not publish my book! He said Count du Laney behaved not at all as a hero should!"

"Oh, dear! *That* doesn't sound very promising," said Anne sympathetically. "Did he tell you *why* he thought Count du Laney was not so very heroic?"

Nerissa wasn't at all sure she wanted to repeat Mr. Heble's judgments concerning the novel she had penned. She and Anne were as close as sisters could be in age, temperament, and feeling. They shared the same passion for romantic stories of gothic proportions. But Nerissa was more deeply disappointed that her work would not be published than she was willing even to let Anne know. In Mr. Heble's polite but firm words of rejection, all her self-esteem—as well as all her plans for the future—was at once reduced to little more than rubble at her feet.

She said in an uncharacteristically forlorn voice, "He had much to say on the matter! Mr. Heble thought the hero should be more proud, more forceful and determined. Anne, you have read my story and liked it very well. I'm sure *you* never considered that a hero should be so!"

Anne averted her eyes and said rather reluctantly, "Well . . . perhaps your hero could have behaved with a *bit* more dash."

"So! I see you agree with Mr. Heble!" said Nerissa, casting her sister a look of injured betrayal. "Rather Trojan behavior of you, I must say! And all this time I thought you *enjoyed* reading my stories!"

"But I do!" said Anne quickly. "They are always so entertaining and quite wonderful. Ever since we were children you've scribbled the most remarkable fairy tales, and I've enjoyed reading them all. You're so clever, I just know you will sell a book one day—if not this book, Rissa dear, then certainly another one!"

Nerissa looked down at the sheaf of pages in her lap on which she had inscribed in carefully crafted copperplate a tale of romantic derring-do. The sight of it sent her spirits plummeting. "I shall never write another story as long as I live!" she said in a voice of passion.

"Not even after hearing Mr. Heble's words of encouragement?"

Nerissa suffered the odd notion that her sister had not listened to a single word she had said. "He was hardly encouraging! He said the hero was not forceful enough and needed to be a bit of a swaggerer! He would have me write Count du Laney as a handsome, strong, daring rogue who hides behind a façade of polished detachment!''

"Now, *that* sounds like a hero," said Anne approvingly. "Is that how Mr. Heble said your hero should be?"

Nerissa nodded.

"I know I'm not very clever about these things, dearest Rissa, but it does seem to me that you have simply to change the hero in your story as Mr. Heble suggested and you shall be quite happily published."

"It is not as simple as you make it sound," said Nerissa. "I *have* changed him—so many times and in so many ways—and *still* I have not written him well!"

"Could you not try again?"

"I shall only fail again," said Nerissa in a voice of flat despair.

"I've never heard you speak so before!" said Anne bracingly. "Of all the five Raleigh sisters, you have always been the determined one. Never have I known you to fail at anything you've set your hand to."

Nerissa turned her head away to gather together a bit of self-control and deliberately concentrated on the crush of traffic surrounding their carriage. Few people of society were in London at this time of year. In the winter months Cits and tradesmen held free reign over the city and its more fashionable haunts until the nobles and gentry began to arrive for the Parliamentary session that opened after the first of the year.

A light dusting of snow had fallen overnight, but the day had warmed enough to have melted the snow down to rather manageable puddles. Nerissa absently watched the passersby skirt the standing pools of water as they went about their business, but when she suddenly realized she and her sister were attracting quite a few curious and some vulgarly bold stares, she dragged her gaze from the window and turned her attention back to her most pressing concern.

"You're right, of course!" she said, clasping her hands together in her lap. "It's wrong of me to cry defeat so easily. But, Anne, I am so very disappointed my book was not purchased! If I may not sell my story, I shall have no means of supporting myself and I shall be forced to find a husband after all!"

"Being married is not so very bad," said Anne gently.

"Perhaps not for you, for Arthur is rather pleasant and he makes no demands on you. But you must agree, our other sisters have not been so fortunate in marriage. In fact, of all our acquaintances, I have never known anyone to be truly happy in marriage—or in love."

"Marriage has nothing to do with love or happiness," said Anne in a voice of quiet authority. "Marriage is merely for the purpose of alliance. At least, that is how Mama explained it to me. Mama said love and romance are found only within the pages of a novel. But a lady may consider herself fortunate to have a husband she respects."

Nerissa cast her a pointed look. "Do you respect Arthur?"

"Well, he is very kind to me," said Anne after a moment's consideration. "And he does give me carte blanche at all the most fashionable shops."

"That's not love," said Nerissa. "At least, not according to all the romantic novels you and I have read. If Arthur were indeed in love with you, he would be something of a bounder, with scores of mistresses and a tragic, deep, dark secret. And only you, with your undying devotion, could reform him."

"I'm not entirely certain," said Anne, "but I don't think such books are to be recognized as authority on the subject."

"My book shall be!" declared Nerissa.

Anne gave a short laugh. "My dear sister! You are barely nineteen years! What, pray, do you know of men and love?"

"Well, you are one and twenty and you have never been in love either," said Nerissa with unerring accuracy.

"True, but only because I was promised to marry Arthur before the end of my first season," Anne said calmly, "and Arthur and I have been married little less than a year, so we really haven't had time to form a deep affection. You shall share the same fate, Rissa dear. All the Raleigh sisters married within a year of their curtsies, and if Mama is to have her way, you shall prove no exception."

Nerissa's fine lips briefly pursed together into a line of determination before she said, "That, however, is exactly what I intend to be! You know, when I was a little girl, I often thought it a cruel twist of fate to have been born the youngest Raleigh daughter. But that was before I realized that I could learn much from my elder sisters—and I have learned by their example that marriage is not for me! Everyone of you was forced to marry a man she didn't not love and hardly knew. *I* will not suffer the same fate," she said with true determination. "Not me!"

She had come close to having her wish. Lady Raleigh's health, always indifferent, had declined enough in the last year to make it impossible for her to orchestrate a fifth and final court presentation for her youngest daughter. Still, she would not hear of allowing Nerissa to remain at home, but promptly packed Nerissa aboard the traveling chaise and sent her off to London to gain a bit of town polish under the aegis of her sister Anne.

Since Anne's husband, Lord Arthur Bridgewater, was a member of the House of Lords and took most seriously his responsibilities in that august assembly, he made it his habit to open his London house in December to prepare for the Parliamentary session that would begin in January. And since Arthur's politics kept him quite occupied, Anne was glad to have her younger sister on hand to keep her company.

Anne gave her sister's hand a gentle squeeze of affection. "I hope you may get your wish, dear Rissa."

"I hope so too, for I am more determined than ever that I shall not marry. But if my book is not published, how am I to support myself? I have no trade and no skills or arts to speak of. Will I, too, wind up in a loveless union?"

Anne patted her hand encouragingly. "You have merely to try again. I think, dearest, you are closer to selling your story than you may know. Simply change your hero in the piece, as Mr. Heble instructed!"

"I shall do my best, but I never considered that a hero could be so difficult!" said Nerissa. "I have tried to write Count du Laney as proud before, and ended in making him merely arrogant. And when I have tried in the past to write him as daring, he has ended as little more than reckless."

"You must try yet again, Rissa dear. This time I know you shall succeed." Anne cast her sister an encouraging smile. "When your novel is published, you shall be more famous than Lady Caroline Lamb. Your book shall rival *Glenarvon* and readers shall swoon to think that such a hero as Count du Laney may exist!"

"I only wish he *did* exist!" said Nerissa with a sigh. "Then I might pattern my story's hero after him, and I shouldn't be in this predicament."

"You might use Arthur for your pattern," offered Anne helpfully.

Nerissa shook her head. Sir Arthur Bridgewater was a young man who treated Anne with kindness, but he was hardly the model for the ideal romantic hero. In fact, now that she came to consider it, Nerissa realized that none of the gentlemen of her acquaintance could possibly timber up to a hero's weight.

"Thank you for offering Arthur, but I do not think he shall serve my purpose. I think my model must be someone more dashing and daring, and rather roguish," she said, doing her best to conjure the image of a man who could remain swaggeringly aloof yet still incite the kind of deep, passionate love she had read about in the chronicles of the Minerva Press.

"Do you mean, someone like *him?*" Anne asked, gesturing out the carriage window toward the far end of the street with a slight ladylike wave of her gloved hand.

Nerissa followed her gaze and caught sight of a gentleman tooling a sporting curricle with deft precision through the crush of traffic.

The pair of grays that pulled his equipage were large beasts with broad chests and thighs and perfectly arched necks that hinted at a barely concealed power. The gentleman driving the curricle appeared to share those same characteristics.

His expression held a wealth of determination as he nimbly guided his grays through the crowd, and, like his horses, he appeared impatient to be off. His eyes and his hair were indistinguishable beneath the shadowing brim of the tall, silk beaver hat he wore. His black, many-caped driving cloak swirled gently behind him in the direction of the liveried tiger perched up behind, and when he looped the reins and poised his whip to overtake a ponderous lozenge coach, he did so with an unmistakable flair.

"Do you see him, Rissa?" asked Anne.

She did indeed, and she was rather mesmerized by the picture he presented. She said in a tone of wonder, "Why, he needs only a patch over one eye and a horrid scar upon his cheek, and he could very well pass for Count du Laney himself! Anne, who *is* he?"

"I have no idea. I don't believe I have ever seen him before."

"I am sure you would have remembered if you had," said Nerissa, her gaze never wavering form the picture he created. "He is the very image of Mr. Heble's description of how a hero should be! I *must* know who he is."

Anne's smooth brow furrowed slightly. "I don't know

how we may discover his identity unless we follow him and see where he goes."

"Do you think we ought?" asked Nerissa, clearly tempted by the idea. She did not wait for an answer, but leaned forward to give the back of the coachman's box a hearty rap. "Coachman! Coachman, follow that curricle!" she called.

"Rissa! You cannot mean to follow that man through the streets of London!" said Anne, horrified by the very notion as the barouche made a sudden lurch forward.

"But I must know who he is! Do tell your coachman to hurry, or we shall lose sight of him in the crush of traffic," said Nerissa, doing her best to keep the fast-fading curricle in view.

"Nerissa Raleigh, if you put your head out the window of this carriage, I shall faint dead away from shame!" exclaimed Anne in a scandalized tone. "You must sit down and calm yourself!"

"I have to make sure we don't lose him in this traffic," said Nerissa reasonably.

"And what, pray, do you intend to do once we catch up to him?"

"I—I don't know," she replied, never having considered the matter that thoroughly. "I dare say I shall merely watch where he goes or see what he does. I'm sure he is on his way even now to some very herolike destination!"

Anne looked doubtful. "He may be criminal for all we know."

"With those horses? A criminal would never have such a bang-up pair in hand!"

"Someday you must tell me how you came by such language," said Anne, trying to sound severe at the very moment the carriage swept around a turn and she was obliged to clutch at the window frame to keep her balance. "Mama would swoon to hear you speak so."

"Don't scold me now, but tell your coachman to go faster!" begged Nerissa as she watched the driver negotiate his speeding curricle around another turn to make his way down yet another street.

Instead of following at the same breakneck pace, the ladies' barouche slowed considerably and then came to a complete halt.

"Why do we stop?" Nerissa demanded in a voice of alarm. "Anne, tell your coachman to drive on!"

"I don't see how he may," said Anne, looking out the windows of first one side then the other of the carriage. "We're quite caught up in a crush, Rissa dear. Until the traffic clears about us, we cannot continue on."

Nerissa, her gaze firmly fixed upon the driver of the curricle, noticed that he, too, had slowed his pace considerably. But he was still moving, however slowly, forward, while the oversized barouche with the Bridgewater crest in which the ladies were traveling had come to a complete halt. She gave another rap on the coachman's box and opened the carriage door. "Then we'll walk," she declared, barely allowing enough time for a groom to rush forward to make a step before she alit to the street.

She turned back to see Anne watching her from the carriage doorway with a horrified expression.

"Nerissa Raleigh, you must be mad! A young lady of breeding does not walk unaccompanied in Piccadilly!"

"Then you must come with me!" replied Nerissa. She did not wait for an answer, but lifted her skirts to step over a rather treacherous puddle and began to pick her way through the tangle of vehicles, riders, and pedestrians toward the shop walk.

Anne hesitated, torn between the compelling need to lend her sister escort and the scandalous prospect of walking about the streets of London without a proper escort or maid. "Nerissa, this is madness! Have you no idea how to go on?"

"Yes, I do! But going on properly has not gotten my book published. If I am to make my living as an authoress,

I must rewrite my hero—and I need *that* man as the model! Please do hurry, Anne, or we shall lose sight of him!''

Anne suppressed the nagging sense of decorum that warned her against following her sister, and carefully stepped down from the coach.

Chapter 2

Nerissa led the way through the snarl of pedestrians strolling before the storefronts. Anne followed close behind, all the while casting nervous glances over her shoulder, lest she be recognized by any of the passersby.

"What if someone sees us?" she asked quite worriedly.

Nerissa reached back to grasp Anne's hand and pull her inexorably forward. "Don't be silly—Cits and tradesmen? *We* don't know any of these people!"

Anne could not be comforted. "I do hope Arthur never learns of this! I shudder to think what he might say!"

"Don't be such a faintheart!" said Nerissa bracingly. "How can you think of Arthur now, when the very epitome of Count du Laney is driving out of my life forever? I shall never again have such an opportunity as this! Only see how all the other vehicles move out of his way! Why, he's absolutely compelling!"

He was also moving quite steadily toward the rise at Piccadilly, and Anne was having a difficult time catching her breath in her attempts to keep pace with both Nerissa and the curricle. "Rissa dear, you must slow down!" she begged, her breath coming in short bursts. "Heavens, next you shall have us running!"

But Nerissa was too intent upon the man in the curricle to heed her sister's words. When the curricle driver slowed to pass yet another vehicle, she found herself almost abreast of him. "Only see how square his jaw is—that is a sure sign of wickedness, I believe!" she said in a tone of deep appreciation. "And he holds his head at such a proud, arrogant angle! If we could manage to get a little closer, I might be able to determine the color of his eyes."

The curricle driver obliged by cutting directly across the ladies' path and sweeping elegantly around the next corner and down the adjoining street.

Nerissa's color heightened slightly from the exertion and excitement of her pursuit. "Oh, Anne, he went past so quickly, I couldn't see his eyes at all!"

"His hair appeared to have been a very lovely brown," said Anne helpfully.

"The color of his hair is of no import at all!" said Nerissa, somewhat impatient with her sister's lack of understanding. "It is his eyes and his demeanor that shall give me the insight I need into his character, not his hair color. We shall just have to catch up to him again," she added with renewed determination. "I shall follow him all day if need be."

"Not down that street, you won't!" said Anne firmly. A protest formed on Nerissa's lips, but Anne cut her off, saying, "He has turned down St. James's Street. No lady of breeding would even consider driving down St. James's—to say nothing of walking!"

Nerissa watched the broad back of the curricle driver fade as he traveled the length of that forbidden street. A small rush of panic enveloped her. "Anne, he's getting away! Are—are you *quite* sure we cannot follow him?"

"Quite," said Anne in a tone that invited no argument. "The street is filled with gentlemen's clubs. My dear sister, you would have to be lost to all reason to attempt to walk down that avenue! You would be ogled and leered at and made the object of the coarsest attentions!"

Nerissa didn't think that being ogled would prove as horrid a fate as Anne made it sound. But she was torn between the note of scandal in her sister's voice and the prospect of never again seeing the curricle driver.

"I don't even know his name! How am I to use him as the model for my hero if I know nothing about him?"

"I suppose you shall have to use your very fertile imagination," said Anne as the Bridgewater barouche drew alongside them at the curb. "Do get in the carriage before we are seen by someone we know!"

But Nerissa didn't move. Instead, her gaze was focused on a very elegantly but conservatively dressed young man who stood contemplating them from the opposite curb.

"Too late," said Nerissa, catching at Anne's sleeve to draw her attention toward the young man, who began to make his way purposefully toward them across the crowded street. "I think we have been discovered."

"Good heavens, it's Arthur!" breathed Anne. "Now we are quite undone!"

Nerissa watched Lord Arthur Bridgewater draw ever nearer and decided she could determine no anger or displeasure in his expression. She said to her sister, "Pooh! You are fretting over nothing. Arthur doesn't look the least bit displeased. Besides, we have done nothing wrong."

Anne drew a deep breath and said in a quick, nervous tone, "Arthur shall be upon us in a mere moment. You must promise me you shall not say a word! Of course what we have done is wrong, but I fear you are too young to realize! I should never have allowed you to embark upon this mad escapade of yours! I have no one to blame but myself!"

She had no chance to say more, for Lord Arthur Bridgewater gained their side. He greeted his wife and sister-in-law with a touch of his gloved hand to the brim of his hat and a slight gesture toward the waiting barouche.

Nerissa climbed aboard and settled most comfortably beside Anne, while Arthur issued instructions for the coachman to drive to Bridgewater House. Then he, too, entered the carriage and took the seat opposite them.

As they crossed the intersection of St. James's, Nerissa couldn't help but cast a rather hopeful look down the length of that street. The curricle driver who so exactly fit the image of the gothic hero of her imagination was nowhere to be seen.

She simply *had* to learn the man's identity, and had the sudden thought that perhaps Arthur might be acquainted with the man in question.

But one look into Arthur's face and the notion of asking him about the curricle driver fled. In the close confines of the barouche, Nerissa could see that his expression revealed a very subtle yet evident displeasure.

Lord Arthur Bridgewater was not generally a man given to emotion. He was only six-and-twenty summers, but an assured manner born of a strong sense of reserve caused him to be mistaken for a man of many more years.

He rested both hands on the hilt of the walking stick poised before him and directed a calm, yet unnerving gaze upon the ladies.

"Imagine my surprise at seeing you just now," he said in an even tone. "At first I thought you must be in need of assistance, that perhaps the barouche had met with an accident."

Anne gave a nervous trill of laughter. "Oh, no! Nothing like that, I assure you!"

"I see. Perhaps, then, you will be good enough to tell me what you were about just now."

He waited very patiently for a reply, and continued to direct his unwavering gaze toward Anne.

She blushed and stammered. "We were—we were merely walking. We weren't about anything particular."

He looked from Anne to Nerissa and back to Anne. "Merely walking?"

"Yes, indeed!" replied Anne, and she nudged her sister. "Weren't we merely walking, dear?"

"It's true, Arthur," said Nerissa. "And I don't really see that we have done anything wrong."

Arthur frowned slightly. "Walking down Piccadilly unattended? Standing at the corner of St. James's Street as if you were common vendors of some sort? My dear Anne, what were you thinking?"

"Please don't scold Anne, for it wasn't her fault at all," said Nerissa, eagerly rushing to her sister's defense. "The whole business was my idea. You see, I was following a man in a curricle and Anne was merely lending me her escort."

Anne clasped her sister's hand in a deathly grip to warn her against saying more, but her effort came too late.

Arthur, his attention kindled, looked from one to the other. "You were following a *man?* A stranger? On a public street? Good God, madam, have you lost all sense of propriety?"

"I am sorry," said Anne, divining most correctly that his last question had been directed toward her. "It was just a lark, and I alone am to blame. Please don't be vexed with Nerissa. She didn't know! *I* could have put a stop to it but didn't. I—I promise it won't happen again."

"I should heartily think so," he said, fixing a stern eye upon her. She wilted a bit under his gaze, and he relented slightly, saying in a much gentler tone, "My dear Anne, this sort of thing will not do—especially now, when my work in the House of Lords is of the greatest import!"

"But it wasn't Anne's fault," said Nerissa, ignoring the urgent tattoo of Anne's fingers squeezing hers. "The whole escapade was my idea entirely. You see, I saw the curricle driver and I simply *had* to follow him, for he was the very image of—"

Arthur raised one gloved hand from the hilt of his cane to halt her words. "I beg you will not trouble yourself further, for there could be no acceptable explanation for your conduct," he said in an even but compelling voice.

"It is insupportable. My position simply will not bear such conduct. Have I not explained all of this to you before, Anne?"

Anne nodded slightly. "Yes, you did *try,* but I understood only half the things you said. I'm afraid I have no turn for politics!"

"One needn't have a turn for politics to understand that my conduct and the conduct of those about me must be of the highest order. Like it or not, you have married a politician, madam, and you must conduct yourself as a politician's wife. And you, my dear sister-in-law," he said, directing a very stern glance toward Nerissa, "must conduct yourself with the utmost propriety during your stay with us."

Nerissa did her best to look contrite. "I understand," she said solemnly.

"Mark me, I shall be watching you at the reception tonight," he warned. "At the first hint of nonsense, I shall insist we leave!"

"You needn't worry, Arthur!" Nerissa assured him quickly. "I shall be the pink of decorum! After all, I wouldn't want to miss any part of my first London assembly. Shall we meet anyone famous there? The Regent, perhaps? Or Lady Caroline Lamb? She's a particular favorite of mine, because of her splendid book!"

Arthur frowned again and said in a slow, measured voice, "The reception is being hosted by Lord and Lady Kendrew—very high in the instep!—and they would no more consider inviting Lady Caroline Lamb than they would a goat. As for the Regent—no, I doubt very much you shall find him attending tonight's reception. It is enough of an honor that we find ourselves invited."

"Lord Kendrew," said Anne informatively, "has been a particular critic of Arthur's since he was first named junior lord of the Treasury. He believes Arthur is too young and does not have the proper political connections and family alliances."

"You understand, then, there can be no foul-ups of any sort tonight," said Arthur. "No rash conduct. No chasing strange men about the place."

"I shan't disappoint you, Arthur," Nerissa promised. "Tonight at the reception I shall be propriety itself."

Arthur looked at her appraisingly for a moment and seemed to be satisfied by the sincerity of her words. He relaxed and smiled kindly upon the ladies as their carriage continued to wend its way through the streets of London.

But Nerissa could not relax. She wanted very much to ask Arthur if he was at all acquainted with the curricle driver, but a pressing desire to sustain Arthur's good humor and avoid another lecture caused her to think better of it. For then.

But just because she didn't mention the man in the curricle didn't mean that he wasn't foremost in her thoughts. A vision of him, assured and aloof as he maneuvered his magnificent horses through the carts and pedestrians along St. James's, teased her. His image swam before her eyes as she tried to rest on her bed that afternoon, and as she dressed that evening in preparation for the reception, she couldn't help but wish that rather than standing at a receiving line, she could stand at the corner of St. James's Street on the chance that the curricle driver sweep past.

Just as Nerissa was entertaining such thoughts, her elusive curricle driver was sweeping instead up the grand staircase of Kendrew House.

He cut an impressive figure as he ascended the steps, and several guests who just happened to be on hand in the grand hall stopped in their tracks to watch his approach. He was dressed in the first stare of fashion, to which he had somehow managed to lend a style all his own. His coat had been cut by a master and fitted him like a glove; his neckcloth was perfectly arranged; and from his starched collar to the high polish of his evening shoes, he presented a lesson in elegance.

Lady Kendrew was installed at the top of the stairs with her son, Lord Crompton, at her side, ready to welcome her guests. Under any other circumstance, she might have swelled with pride at seeing such a leader of fashion present himself at one of her functions. Instead, she watched his approach with mounting annoyance.

He cleared the last step and she greeted him with a voice of ice. "Nephew! What, pray, are you doing here?"

"You invited me," he said, one brow flying with interest. "In fact, you wrote my sister-in-law and begged her to persuade me to come, didn't you?"

"Yes, but I didn't intend that you should arrive now! You are much too early! And if you arrive early, you shall surely leave early!"

"That is exactly my intention!" He saw her color rise and smiled slightly. "Aunt, you know I have no interest in this sort of thing."

"But if you leave before most of my guests arrive, no one shall know you were ever here!"

"That suits me just fine. I can't have it put about town that I've taken an interest in politics, can I?"

"Oh, no! Not you!" retorted Lady Kendrew, her temper rising along with the tenor of her voice. "You would rather feed the flame of rumor that you're nothing but a worthless fribble! Never mind what damage such talk may do to the family!"

He had been about to move on, to greet Lord Crompton, who had been standing by, watching with growing concern the interplay between aunt and nephew. But at this, the curricle driver stopped and cast a look back at Lady Kendrew.

"You give me more credit than I deserve, Aunt. As you have so often reminded me, we Davenants are above reproach. Aren't you always fond of telling people that we have a duke, a marquess, and two earls in the family? With such a noble bloodline, I doubt I could ever do the family very much harm—although I feel it my duty to try!"

Lady Kendrew took a deep and steadying breath. "If you have an ounce of affection for me, you shall go home now and come back again later."

"Can't," he said bluntly. "I've got an engagement later." He threw a negligent glance over his shoulder and added, "And you've got guests arriving, I see. Crompton, be good enough to direct me to the champagne!"

Lord Crompton thought it a very good notion to put as much distance as possible between his mother and his cousin. He led him away toward the reception hall, saying, "I'd ask what the deuce you meant by speaking to my mother so, but I dare say I can guess the answer!"

"Can you?" He looked at his cousin down the length of his nose.

"You came—and early too—just to cut up my mother. She'll have a storm in her bonnet the rest of the evening because of you."

"Then she shouldn't have invited me—or applied to my sister-in-law to pressure me to come," Mr. Davenant said simply.

Lord Crompton was a young man who would have very much liked to cultivate his cousin's good opinion. Mr. Davenant was, after all, a rather feared leader of fashion, and he had been known to make or break a reputation merely by lifting his eyebrow. The only other person Lord Crompton could think of whose opinion might have carried more weight was very likely Mr. Davenant's sister-in-law, the present Marchioness of Pankhurst. Between the two of them, they held the fashionable world in thrall—one by means of an arrogant recklessness toward convention that had vanquished even the most determined hostess, the other with a regal graciousness and beauty that had been her trademark since she first made her entrance in society as a girl.

Lady Kendrew was certainly a member of the very same family that had produced two such shining beacons of fashionable light, but Lord Crompton was very well aware that his mother would never soar to the same societal heights as Mr. Davenant or Lady Pankhurst. While she still enjoyed the cache of being a Davenant, she would never be able to claim the same degree of social success enjoyed by those two members of the family.

He had often felt a little sorry that his mother and her efforts would go so unrewarded, and he didn't think his cousin was being at all helpful in the matter.

Unlike his mother, his lordship was neither dependent upon Mr. Davenant nor afraid of him. But he lacked a good deal of Mr. Davenant's confidence and often found himself being made to feel the fool whenever they were in company together. So far, this evening had proved to be no exception.

"My mother," said Lord Crompton, "would give her eyeteeth to own the kind of influence over society you or your sister-in-law wields. If my mother applied to the marchioness to force you to come tonight, it is only because she wants the evening to be a success. She wants to be seen in your company."

"It wouldn't do you any harm either," said Mr. Davenant with unnerving directness. He accepted a glass of champagne from a bowing servant. "I shouldn't worry too much about your mother, Crompton. I shall do my duty by her: I shall nod and smile at her guests, and when I become intolerably bored—as I assure you, I shall!—I'll make certain to hide my yawns behind the back of my hand."

"Then—then, do I have your promise you shall stay long enough to ensure the success of her party?"

"I promise nothing of the kind—unless, of course, there is to be cards or some sort of entertainment got up?"

Lord Crompton frowned. "But—but this evening is a political reception, for heaven's sake! The only entertainment to be had is conversation!"

"I can't think of anything that could be *less* entertaining!" said Mr. Davenant with distaste.

"I suppose I could speak to my father. We might set up

a card table or two in one of the saloons . . ." said Lord Crompton thoughtfully.

"Manage it, Cousin! In the meantime I shall see what I can do to occupy myself in your mother's reception hall."

"You'll promise not to leave, won't you? I'll expect to find you here when I return!"

Mr. Davenant allowed his gaze to wander over the clutch of guests assembled in the long hall. Almost he refused; almost he announced that he had changed his mind and had decided to leave after all; but as his eyes scanned the assembly, his attention was caught by a face that was familiar to him.

On the far side of the room, he recognized a woman, an old flirt—he couldn't quite recall her name—he remembered very vividly, having a lively wit and an undeniable charm.

He took a fortifying sip of champagne. "Yes, I promise! And when you have a card table arranged, Cousin, you shall find me here. I see a familiar face in this crowd, and I think I shall pass a very agreeable time renewing our acquaintance. Yes, a very agreeable time indeed!"

Chapter 3

It wasn't until later that evening, when the Bridgewater party arrived at Lord and Lady Kendrew's town house, that all thoughts of the curricle driver were at last pushed from Nerissa's mind. She had never before attended a gathering of any kind among the London Fashionables, and she found herself quite dazzled by the splendors of Kendrew House.

Upon their entrance, Nerissa and Anne were escorted to a small room, where they divested themselves of their cloaks and bonnets, and set about repairing any wrinkles and creases to their gowns before they presented themselves to their host and hostess.

"Will there be dancing here tonight, do you think?" Nerissa asked as she checked her appearance in an oversized looking-glass that stood in one corner of the room.

"No, this is a reception, not a ball. Even more important, it is a *political* reception. I'm afraid Arthur attends quite a few of these gatherings, and, of course, as his wife, I must attend too."

"It doesn't sound as if they are very entertaining,"

said Nerissa, interpreting her sister's rather forlorn expression.

"They're not, believe me! Arthur shall spend the entire evening speaking of this bill or that law, and I must remain by his side and smile and pretend to understand what everyone is saying. I wish I were more clever about these things!"

"Nonsense! You are quite clever, Anne. The problem, I fear, is that Arthur is rather dull."

Anne accepted this pronouncement as one she herself had often conceded. "I know," she said rather dismally. "But he does treat me with kindness. This morning, for instance, he might have raved over our conduct and read us a curtain lecture, but he didn't. He has always been very gentle with me, I think, and yet . . ." Anne gave the matter a moment's thought before she went on. "And yet I should so like him to be a bit more romantic! A bit more like your curricle driver."

Nerissa laughed slightly and gave her sister an affectionate kiss on the cheek. "There are times when I fear you are even more of a romantic than I am! Perhaps one day Arthur shall learn to behave with a bit more flair!"

"Then I must hope that day is not far off. In the meantime, I shall do my duty and try to enjoy being a politician's wife," Anne said as she and Nerissa joined Arthur, and together they entered the reception hall.

The greetings they received from Lord and Lady Kendrew were cordial yet cold. Lord Kendrew welcomed them in a very formal, stately way that invited no conversation. Lady Kendrew, upon her introduction to Nerissa, favored her with a hard stare that swept appraisingly over her person, and she held out her hand with only two rather limp fingers extended.

Nerissa touched her fingers briefly, dipped a curtsy, and said, "I am very pleased to meet you, ma'am. Thank you so much for including me in your invitation."

Her hostess responded with a rather rigid "How do you do" before she turned in a rather deliberate fashion to greet another guest.

Nerissa was left with the distinct impression that Lord and Lady Kendrew would wish her otherwhere than in their reception hall. The notion was rather upsetting. "Do you think I shouldn't have come with you?" she hissed into Anne's ear as they made their way into the sea of guests.

Arthur overheard her and said, "Why? Because of Lord and Lady Kendrew's demeanor? Don't consider it."

"Lady Kendrew always behaves that way," said Anne. "She has never been any other but cold to me or to Arthur. She rather frightens me."

"But if they don't want you here in their home, why do they invite you?" Nerissa asked.

"This is politics," said Arthur reasonably. "Lord Kendrew must invite me because I hold too much influence to be ignored. And I must accept his invitation because Lord Kendrew has too much power for me to do otherwise."

"It seems a very unhappy way to spend an evening," said Nerissa, divining that her immediate future would hold little opportunity for entertainment.

Anne slipped her arm about her sister's shoulders and gave her a quick hug. "It's not so bad. After all, we have to endure only one evening of Lord and Lady Kendrew's treatment. Why, tomorrow they shall not deign to recognize us because we are not of their circle and they mean to keep it that way. You'll see! The next time Lady Kendrew spots us, in the shops or out driving, she shall behave as if she doesn't even recall the acquaintance!"

Nerissa was rather stunned. "Do you mean to tell me Lady Kendrew *snubs* you?"

Arthur nodded. "Rather dreadfully, I'm afraid. And Lord Kendrew speaks to me only when he must in the Lords. Still, this reception tonight is important because of the other guests who are in attendance. Anne and I shall do our best to enjoy ourselves, and accomplish some political good while we are here.''

"You must try to enjoy the evening too, dear Rissa,'' said Anne encouragingly.

"I shall,'' replied Nerissa pessimistically, "although it would be very helpful if there were dancing. It seems a bit odd to invite such a great number of people to a reception, only to have them merely stand about and talk of politics.''

"Lord and Lady Kendrew don't usually host dancing parties, but they do hold this reception every year,'' said Anne as Arthur turned away to speak to a political ally. "It's the first social event in December, and it starts off the Christmas season of parties for the politicos. It's all terribly dull, but it's good for Arthur's career.'' She saw that her husband's attention was captured in conversation with yet another gentleman, and she whispered rather urgently, "Promise me you shall stay close by me tonight. I shall need your liveliness to keep me from withering away from boredom!''

"I'm sure you overexaggerate,'' said Nerissa with a smile. "No reception can be as tedious as you describe!''

But within half an hour of so saying, Nerissa was caused to revise that opinion. Anne had spoken nothing but the truth. Every person standing about the long reception room was speaking of political matters. Nerissa understood little of the various topics that were being discussed. More important, she had no interest in anything that was being said, and she was quite heartily bored.

She overheard another guest mention that a card room had been set up in one of the small parlors just down the hall from the reception. She longed to escape there, but when she whispered that intention to Anne, she received a sharp look in reply.

"Certainly not!'' hissed Anne in a voice low enough that the other guests might not hear. "The card tables are for the gentlemen only. How can you possibly think to join them?''

Disappointed yet obedient, Nerissa remained with Anne at Arthur's side. A little while later, Arthur introduced her to Lord and Lady Kendrew's son, Lord Crompton. He was dressed to a wicket in a coat of blue superfine and a waist-coat of dazzling design. His fobs, rings, and pins were displayed in perfect arrangement, and he projected, for all purposes, the very image of a fashionable man-about-town.

Nerissa thought him quite a handsome young man, but she noticed, too, that his manners, while correct, fell just short of pleasing. Like his parents, he greeted the Bridgewaters most coolly, and when Arthur made him known to Nerissa, he barely nodded and uttered only a mildly convincing welcome.

Arthur attempted to engage him in conversation and made some very general observations to which Anne added at intervals her rather shy but enthusiastic agreement. But to everything they said, Lord Crompton replied in a politely tolerant manner that did more to hinder the conversation than encourage it.

To watch her brother-in-law strive so diligently to engage him in conversation and to see her sister smile so hopefully upon his lordship, only to be treated in such a fashion, made Nerissa most uncomfortable and rather angry.

As soon as Lord Crompton moved away to speak to another guest, she said in a lowered voice, ''Must you suffer such treatment from everyone in London? Or just the people of this household?''

''Please don't be upset by the behavior of the Kendrews or Lord Crompton, Rissa dear,'' said Anne.

''We warned you that we were not of their set,'' said Arthur quite reasonably. ''And while Kendrew had to invite us tonight, he and Lady Kendrew mean to warn us off expecting any other invitations.''

''But why? Why do they dislike you so?'' asked Nerissa,

deeply confused. "After all, you're a very clever man, Arthur, and Anne is sweetness itself."

"As I said before, this is politics," said Arthur. "You see, I was appointed to the treasury bench instead of the man Kendrew would have chosen. Mine is a position of power and influence and, I am sorry to say, I have had to wield that influence one or two times in a manner Kendrew would have had otherwise."

"So he snubs you for it!" said Nerissa, a good deal disgusted.

"He can do little else. Truly, no harm is done—to me at any rate. But I think your sister suffers more than I do," he said with an insight that surprised his wife.

She blushed slightly. "It is true. Lady Kendrew has closed all society's doors that might have been opened to me. I should love to attend the very best parties and balls, but without Lady Kendrew's countenance, I am afraid my social circle is rather limited."

Nerissa considered that if all Lady Kendrew's balls and parties were as tedious as this one, she would not be at all disappointed to find herself excluded from the guest list. But there was no denying that Anne was more deeply hurt by Lady Kendrew's cruelty than she was willing to admit.

In fact, the entire evening was proving to be very uncomfortable, what with ungracious hosts and tedious conversation. Nerissa was beginning to believe there could be no expedient end to her suffering, and she cast her wide brown eyes about the room, as if seeking out possible avenues of escape.

That's when she spied him. The curricle driver. She was sure it was he, and her attention flared.

He was standing at the far side of the room, engaged in conversation with an elegant woman of great beauty and impeccable fashion. In the candlelight of the reception room, his hair shone a deep rich brown and his skin was a trifle dark, as if he were no stranger to the sun and its warmth. The color of his eyes was indistinguishable, but his gaze was firmly focused upon the woman by his side.

Nerissa watched him lean closer to the woman and murmur something of unmistakable intimacy that caused the woman to playfully swat her fan at his thick, well-muscled arm. The woman laughed gaily and made a brief reply.

Nerissa's heart swelled. How elegant he looked! How roguish his behavior! Watching the curricle driver set the beauty to blushing convinced Nerissa more than ever that he was the true embodiment of Count du Laney, the hero in her novel.

She watched the curricle driver take the woman's gloved hand in his and bring it to his lips with a grace that sent Nerissa's own heart to quickening.

He gave a cursory glance about the room. Nerissa's heart thudded against her ribs at the mere thought that for just one brief moment his eyes might meet hers. However, his glance was as quick as it was fleeting.

He directed a slight bow toward the beautiful woman at his side before he left her to make his way about the perimeter of the room.

Before she could give the matter any thought, before she could lose her nerve, Nerissa uttered a hurried and strangled excuse toward Anne and Arthur and set off in pursuit of the curricle driver.

It took some moments for her to gain the other side of the room, for she had to wend her way through the clutches of conversing guests. Then, once she had managed to present herself at the very spot in which she had last seen him, she found that he had moved away yet again.

Nerissa glanced quickly about and saw him striding purposefully toward a door just a little farther on. She had a sudden notion that he was off in search of the card game or some other equally masculine diversion. How like Count du Laney he truly was! Of course he was bored! Surely, she reasoned, a man of his heroic qualities would not tolerate such an insipid reception as this.

Impulsively, she slipped through the very same door behind which she had seen him disappear a mere moment before.

The doorway gave off onto a short hallway, but the curricle driver was nowhere to be seen. Nerissa hesitated a moment, unsure whether to return to the reception hall or continue her search for him. A sudden vision of Anne, standing at the side of a husband she didn't love, and smiling bravely through her boredom, rekindled Nerissa's resolve. To her mind, the elusive curricle driver was her best hope for seeing her book published. If she ever wished to escape the fate Anne suffered, she simply *had* to find him.

She opened the first door off the hallway. Beyond the door was a small salon. She slipped inside the room. No lamps were lit, but a fire was burning in the hearth, and it lent a soft glow to the cozy room. She moved toward the fire and held her hands out against its heat, contemplating the wisdom of following the curricle driver farther down the hall.

She hated the thought of giving up her pursuit of him now, when she was so close to learning his name, so close to observing his very herolike behavior. But she knew that if Arthur were to discover her actions, she would be punished indeed. When the thought occurred to her that Anne, too, might suffer because of her actions, she realized how foolishly she was behaving.

She decided to compromise. She resolved to look for him just once more, to investigate only one more room that let off the hall. If he wasn't in the next room, she promised herself, she would quit her search for him. It would break her heart to do so, but she would quit her search.

No sooner had she reached that decision than she heard

the door slam shut behind her. She turned quickly. Her brown eyes widened with shock and a small mewl of surpise escaped her lips.

Lounging against the closed door, wearing an expression of almost palpable anger, was the curricle driver.

Chapter 4

It took a moment for Nerissa to recover from her initial surprise at finding herself alone with the curricle driver but her confusion quickly gave way to the heady realization that she was at last face-to-face with the man who had so haunted her thoughts for an entire day.

In the close confines of the small sitting room, he was taller than she had supposed he would be, and he wore his finely tailored evening clothes with an unmistakable air of careless sophistication. His complexion was rather dark in the dim light. The dancing flames from the fire in the hearth did not burn bright enough for her to distinguish the color of his eyes, although they did chisel lines of high living across his handsome countenance. His mouth was straight and, at that moment, very grim. His expression was one of daunting anger as he looked at her down the length of his straight nose.

Nerissa drew a long breath and regarded him with deep appreciation. Everything about him—his manner, his dress, his hard, threatening expression—exactly fitted the notion she had formed of a true gothic hero.

There was also about him a ruthlessness to his manner and an unforgivingness to his eye that set her nerves flurrying. She thought of the way he had slammed the door shut and realized, too late, that she was very much alone with a very dangerous-looking man.

She summoned her courage and said with a false show of bravado, "Be so good as to open the door, sir. I—I cannot think it is a wise thing for me to be alone with you."

"You should have thought of that before you came in here," he said in a low, resonant voice. He used his broad shoulders to lever his body away from the door, and he took a few steps toward her.

That simple action set her heart racing. There was an unmistakable air of danger that surrounded his movement and a certain swashbuckling arrogance to his stride.

She had no idea what he intended to do, but she resolved to stand her ground if he should have a notion to advance upon her and prove himself to be more of a bounder than a hero.

"If you think you shall startle or frighten me, you are very much mistaken!" she said in a voice that was more breathless than brave. "Stay where you are and don't come any farther into the room until you have told me what you mean by such uncommon behavior!"

He ignored her words and said instead, in a tone that was just as harsh as his countenance, "Who are you? And why have you been following me?"

Nerissa felt a hot flush of embarrassment fan across her cheeks. So he had noticed! And she thought she had been so careful to have observed him without being discovered. She felt like a schoolgirl caught in some foolish misdeed and gave a falsely bright laugh to cover her discomfort. "Follow you? Why, sir, what—what can you mean?"

He moved a little closer to the fire. Nerissa was at last able to determine the color of his eyes. They were a very light gray color that underscored the coldness of his glance.

"You followed me this morning all the way to St. James's," he said in a low, accusing tone. "You followed me again this evening in the reception hall. Don't trouble yourself to deny it."

"I think you mistake coincidence for design," she said, forcing a light note to her voice. "Heavens, what possible reason could I have for following you?"

His eyes narrowed slightly. "That is exactly what I would like to know. You can either tell me the truth now, young lady, or I can drag you back into that reception and hold you up before the crowd, demanding that someone claim you and tell me your identity."

Her eyes widened slightly. The look he cast her was quite ruthless. She didn't doubt for a moment that he was capable of such a deed.

"There is no need to resort to threats, I assure you! Perhaps I *was* following you," she said a bit reluctantly, "but I did so only with the best of reasons!"

He lifted one brow. "Such as?"

She tried to counter the sudden fluttering of her heart with a nervous titter. "You shall laugh when you hear it," she promised.

"I am prepared to run that risk." He eyed her expectantly as he reached into an inner pocket of his elegantly styled coat and withdrew an enameled box, which he flicked open with a practiced hand.

She thought he meant to take a pinch of snuff, but realized, as his long fingers disappeared amid the contents of the box, that it was longer and slimmer than the snuffboxes she had seen her father use.

As it happened, the box did not contain snuff, for the gentleman extracted from the depths of the elegant little case a narrow brown object that was a little slimmer but about the same length as one of his long, well-manicured fingers.

He brought one end of the object toward his lips, pausing just short of that goal. His hand poised in midair, he looked at her, one brow raised questioningly, and he asked, as if it were an afterthought, "Do you have any objection?"

She hadn't the faintest idea what exactly he was asking permission to do. His manner was so compelling, and she was so fascinated by the prospect of seeing what he intended to do next, that she said quite promptly, "No, no, of course not!"

He moved to the fireplace with loose, long-legged strides and set a kindling stick aglow by dipping it into the flames of the hearth. Then he put one end of the brown cylinder between his finely chiseled lips and lit the other end with the kindling.

Nerissa held her breath, impressed by the extraordinary display she had just been privileged to witness. He was really even more dazzling and herolike than she had dared hope he would be.

He drew a deep breath against the brown cylinder, then took it from his mouth to exhale a delicate ribbon of smoke that danced gracefully toward the ceiling.

She could hardly take her eyes from it. "Lovely!" she murmured appreciatively.

He cocked a brow. "Haven't you ever seen a man smoke before?"

"No, never! Can only men do it?"

"I should think so," he replied, gazing down upon her with a look of mild amusement.

The masculine aroma of tobacco touched her senses, and she eyed him measuringly. He was lounging quite casually against the mantel, one long arm draped comfortably across its length, but she detected a certain intensity that belied his casual pose. There was an unmistakable strength to the coiled muscles of his shoulders and legs, and a haughtiness to the expression on his handsome face that convinced her that he bowed to no one. He was an admirable specimen of a man indeed! So convinced was Nerissa that he was the perfect model for the hero in her book, she could barely take her eyes from him.

She felt inexplicably tongue-tied in his presence. She searched her memory to find some sparkling bit of conversation to offer up. In the end, she could only manage to say, somewhat foolishly, "My father takes snuff."

His gaze upon her upturned face was unwavering. "Indeed?"

"Do you know him? He is Sir Danford Raleigh of Chelsea Hall and I am his youngest daughter. All my elder sisters are married. In fact, I'm the only one who isn't, and I've come to stay with my sister, Anne. She is Lady Bridgewater, you see—"

"My dear young woman! Has anyone ever told you you talk too much?" he interrupted, but with such a charming smile, Nerissa was unable to take the least offense.

She smiled and said impulsively, "Yes! But only when I am nervous. Otherwise I can speak very sensibly, I assure you!"

"Are you nervous now?"

"I am indeed. I have been very eager to become acquainted with you, and it's important I make a good impression so you'll be disposed to help me."

His expression altered subtly. In an instant the look of bland amusement disappeared, and in its place Nerissa saw a shadow of the angry wariness he had worn when first he had entered the room.

"Help you?" he repeated stiffly.

"Yes! I have a simple request, really. It's the reason I've been following you."

"You'd have done better to have chased rainbows instead of me! I'm rarely of a mind to help anyone."

"Not ever? Even if someone is desperate for your help?"

"Especially when someone is desperate for my help," he said emphatically. "Perhaps you had better explain yourself, young woman. Just why have you been following me?"

His expression told her he would not again allow her to evade telling him the truth. Briefly, she considered lying to him, but reason told her she could not possibly profit by such a ploy. Besides, under the weight of his piercing stare, she couldn't come up with a piece of fiction that sounded at all plausible.

"I shall tell you the truth, sir, but first—may I know *your* name?"

He looked at her sharply, surprised by her request. Then he said simply, "Davenant."

She was a little disappointed. "Is that all? Are you simply *Mr.* Davenant? You see, I was rather hoping you were a foreign count or, at the very least, a baronet."

He straightened slightly and said in a rather confounded tone, "I hope you're not too disappointed in me."

"I am a trifle disappointed, but you cannot help it, after all," she allowed handsomely. "It would be better for me, though, if you were perhaps a *bit* more noble."

He inhaled deeply from the cylinder of tobacco and his lip curled slightly; Nerissa couldn't tell if his faint sneer was a reaction to her words or to the swirl of smoke that escaped his lips and coiled up around his aquiline nose.

"I am waiting," he said, "for you to tell me why you have been following me."

Another wave of embarrassment swept over her. She felt foolish and suddenly tongue-tied. The look he cast her didn't make it at all easy for her to reply, but it did make her summon her courage.

She took a deep breath and said gamely, "I followed you because I wanted to observe you. I wanted to see how you behaved and where you went and—and know everything about you."

His gaze was unwavering. "Why?"

"Because you are the perfect, ideal romantic hero," she said in a rush. That explanation, which she had thought so reasonable a mere moment before, now sounded very silly and completely nonsensical.

"Hero?" repeated Mr. Davenant with a frown. "*What* hero?"

"The hero of the novel I have written," said Nerissa. She saw his frown increase and added quickly, "You see, I have written a book, but Mr. Heble, the publisher, will not buy it unless I change the hero to be more daring and dashing!"

"What in the name of Zeus has that to do with me?" demanded Mr. Davenant in a voice of promised thunder.

"*You* are that hero!" said Nerissa quite simply. "I knew it the moment I saw you on the street this morning, driving your curricle with such flair! I thought then that you were the very embodiment of Count du Laney. And tonight, when I saw you with that woman at the reception, and you were flirting so outrageously with her, I realized no other but you could serve as the model for the hero of my book!"

He stiffened, his back going as straight as a plank. "Model for your hero?" he repeated with an appalled expression. "My dear young woman, have you taken leave of your senses?"

"Not at all! I assure you, I am quite sane! It is very important that I have my novel published. But to do so I must change the hero to be—well, to be exactly like you! I should like to observe you, if you don't mind and if it isn't too much trouble."

One look into his face told Nerissa he was more than stunned by her request. She added quickly, "I promise not to be a charge on you! I am very quick to learn, so I shall not have to observe you for very many days, I dare say."

He looked down at her from his position by the fire, and his eyes, for all their laziness, were curiously penetrating. "And I suppose during the time you are observing me, we must be constantly in each other's company."

"It would be very helpful if we were to be so," allowed Nerissa.

"I see," he said in a tone that convinced her he was less than enamored of the scheme. "May I congratulate you on your rather ingenious plot. Very clever. However, you are not the first young woman to have used your imagination to set a trap my direction. Your efforts are wasted, however. Fresh schoolgirls are not in my line.''

Nerissa felt her cheeks color. "Why, I haven't set a trap for you at all! Heavens, I have no wish to *marry* you! I only want to *observe* you!''

"Observe me? Why? So you may best gauge the exact moment when a fit of swoons will put you in the very spot where I shall have no choice but to catch you in my arms? Or so you may best discover the most opportune time to twist your ankle, thus compelling me to lend you my arm for support? You may save yourself the trouble! I'm very well acquainted with every devise and design employed by females with an eye to marrying my fortune!''

"Have you a fortune?" asked Nerissa with interest. "Are you *very* rich?''

He cocked a cynical brow. "Didn't you know?''

"I had no idea, but I'm glad to have learned it now," she said approvingly. "The more I know about you, the more I am convinced that you are exactly as Mr. Heble said a hero should be!''

Mr. Davenant stood very still for a moment and regarded her with frowning concentration. At last he said, "I believe you are quite serious!''

"I'm very determined," she replied. "I simply must have my book published. If I am to make the changes as Mr. Heble asked, you are my only hope.''

"My dear young woman," he said, and the coldness returned to his eyes, "do you really suppose I would agree to such a preposterous scheme?''

Nerissa felt her cheeks color slightly. "Well, yes! Yes, I do!" she said. "Why shouldn't you agree? After all, it will cost you nothing.''

"Nothing but my consequence." He threw the cylinder of tobacco into the fire with unnecessary force and brought himself up to his full commanding height.

"Your consequence?" she repeated. "Do you mean to tell me you move in the very first circles?"

"I contrive to pass myself creditably," he said in a voice that would have quelled the enthusiasm of a lesser person.

Nerissa clasped her hands together. "Then you really *are* the perfect hero!" she said, deeply aware of her good fortune in having found such a man. "What good fortune! I was half convinced you were merely handsome and daring! But now, to discover that you are rich and noble too—you truly *are* the most heroic man I've ever encountered!"

For a moment he looked as if he had been thrown quite off his stride. Then his expression hardened and he said with a hint of anger, "My dear young woman—"

"Please, call me Nerissa!"

"I suggest you try for a little conduct!" He saw that she was looking at him with a rather bewildered expression that was not without its charm. He said in a slightly softer tone, "I shouldn't go about town telling strange men you find them handsome and daring if I were you. No doubt there are those who might find it flattering—I'm not one of them."

"Are—are you telling me you won't help me?" she asked.

"At last! Some proof that you can speak sensibly!"

"But why would you refuse to help? I want only to write about you in my novel."

"Did you really believe I would agree? Me? Breck Davenant? Figuring in a novel? It's unthinkable—especially the absurd tale of derring-do someone of your nature might pen?"

"*My nature?*" Nerissa repeated slowly. "What do you mean?"

"You can't suppose your behavior is at all acceptable! You shouldn't even be here with me now, to say nothing of padding about behind me on the street. I'd wager this isn't the first time you've behaved rashly. And I'd guess you have a taste for the theatrical!"

"I don't often follow men about on the streets," said Nerissa in a rather affronted tone. "But when I saw you, I knew there was something different about you. Oh, I can't explain this very well! Just believe me when I tell you that I have no designs on you and I don't want to marry you! Nor do I want to marry *any*one, for that matter! I merely wish to observe you and write about you, and then you shall never have to see me again."

"No. You shall not observe me and you most assuredly shall not write about me," he said. The darkling tone in his voice told her that further argument would prove useless.

Still, Nerissa couldn't bring herself to abandon hope. "If you won't help me, my book will never be published."

"No doubt Shakespeare and Chaucer would be relieved to know their positions in literature remain unchallenged."

Nerissa felt the flush of mortification cover her cheeks. "You—you needn't be insulting!"

"My dear young woman," he said in an oddly gentle tone, "it is you who has insulted *me!* By thinking I would be foolish enough and careless enough with my reputation to allow you to lampoon it in the pages of your Minerva sheet scribblings."

He crossed to the door and opened it, then eyed her expectantly. "I trust you can find your way back to the reception without my escort."

Only moments before, Nerissa had thought Mr. Davenant the embodiment of her perfect hero. Now he stood looking at her with quite the coldest and most unforgiving eyes she had ever seen. "Then, you *won't* help me!" she said, hardly able to credit that he could be so heartless.

"I believe I have made that quite clear. Now, Miss Raleigh, you will return to the reception. If you are wise, you will take steps to ensure that you and I never have occasion to meet again."

Nerissa tried to gather about her some shreds of dignity

in the face of such a crude dismissal. "I assure you, I shall!" she said, marching up to face him with a bearing that was more stormy than regal. She felt an irrational desire to hurt him as much as his treatment had hurt her. She said witheringly, "If by some chance our paths may cross, Mr. Davenant, I assure you, I—I shall *not* recognize the acquaintance!"

"I shall do my best to bear such a devastating snub," he said as he placed his hand at the small of her back and propelled her into the hallway.

The moment he released her, Nerissa whirled about, only to find that he had silently closed the door behind her.

Her temper warred with a strong sense of mortification. Rashly, she considered opening the door and storming back into the room to accuse him of being rude and heartless and destroying all her plans for the future. Further reflection told her that a man like Mr. Davenant already knew himself to be cruel, and he no doubt reveled in the knowledge.

Nerissa had no choice but to slip back into the reception. She found Anne stoically maintaining her position at Arthur's side while he conferred with his fellow members of the House of Lords on some issue.

Anne shot her a look of concern. "Where have you been?" she asked in whisper, lest her husband should overhear. "I was half afraid Arthur would notice you were missing!"

"I saw *him,*" hissed Nerissa. "The curricle driver."

Anne's eyes widened. "Do not tell me you went after him again," she begged. "Nerissa, how *could* you?"

"Don't scold me now, for I couldn't bear it!" said Nerissa, battling back the sudden pricking of tears behind her eyes. "He was horrid, Anne, and not at all like Count du Laney! Why, he isn't even a noble, but only a *Mr.* Davenant!"

Anne went very still. "Mr. Davenant?" she repeated. "Not Breck Davenant, I hope!"

From the tone of her sister's voice, Nerissa wasn't at all sure she wanted to answer the question. "I—I believe he said that was his first name. Why, Anne? Do you know him? Is he important?"

"Of course he is important! I see now I shall regret to my dying day ever allowing you to chase that curricle!"

"Anne, do you *know* Mr. Davenant?"

"Only by name. Heaven knows, Arthur and I do not travel in the same circle as the Davenant family! I've never met the man, and now I sincerely doubt I ever shall! Oh, Rissa, don't you realize what you've done?"

"No," she answered candidly. "What have I done?"

"Breck Davenant is the grandson of a duke and the brother of a marquess. If only half the stories I've heard of him are true, he's as rich as Croesus and a hundred times more influential!"

"Goodness, I had no idea," said Nerissa thoughtfully, "although he did tell me he was rather wealthy."

"Did he also tell you Lady Kendrew is his aunt?" demanded Anne, at the end of her patience.

"No, but only because he was too busy insulting me. Anne, he absolutely refused to help me with my book!"

Anne shot her a choleric look. "Rissa, don't you understand what this means?"

"Yes, it means I shall not have my book published and I shall be forced to marry after all," said Nerissa in a voice of dramatic despair.

"Do forget that horrid book for a moment, will you?" demanded Anne, her temper flashing. "Don't you realize that if you insulted Mr. Davenant in any way or subjected him to any of your foolishness, we are quite ruined? He has only to snub us or tell his aunt of your behavior and we shall find every fashionable door closed to us."

Nerissa didn't think this an opportune time to tell her sister that Mr. Breck Davenant had already made clear the fact that he didn't intend to recognize them. She said instead, in a very small voice, "I'm sorry."

"I wish you would not behave so impulsively!" said Anne with feeling.

"So do I," said Nerissa, realizing, rather forlornly, where her actions had gotten her. "Indeed, so do I!"

Chapter 5

George Edward Cambreck Davenant whipped his curricle around the next corner with all the speed, agility, and potential for danger that made his tiger swell admiringly.

"Very nicely took, Mr. Breck," said the tiger approvingly from his perch up behind his master. He let loose one hand from its grip on the curricle to draw his knitted wool muffler a bit closer about his throat and ears. Their speed of travel lent the December air a stinging quality, but he wouldn't dream of begging his master to slow his course. Only Breck Davenant drove a pair with such style. A sudden swell of emotion curiously akin to paternal pride enveloped the tiger, and he said, "There's not another man in England with lead hands like yours."

Breck Davenant didn't reply for a moment as he concentrated on weaving his vehicle through a jam of vendor carts that littered almost an entire London street. As soon as he had maneuvered clear, he said in a provocative tone, "That is because I am the stuff of heroes!"

If his tiger disagreed, he chose not to show it. "If you say so, Mr. Breck."

"And I have it on good authority that I drive my curricle with a certain flair!"

"None better to know that than me, sir."

"Damn your impudence, Henry! Aren't you the least bit impressed with me?" demanded Breck in a laughing voice. "I'll have you know, I met a young lady last evening and *she* thinks me the epitome of a storybook hero!"

"Any man who can control the kind of prime cattle you own is no doubt worthy of the praise," said his tiger mildly.

Breck raised one rather sardonic brow. "Since you are the one who first taught me to drive, I wonder, Henry, which of us you are indeed praising!"

"Now, Mr. Breck," the tiger replied in a cajoling tone that only a long-time employee might be forgiven using. "You're a fine driver in your own right and I dare say you know many more things about driving than I ever taught you. Just mind the ice on the road and keep an eye to the dog behind that job cart on your right, if you please."

Since Breck knew himself to be generally accounted something of a top-sawyer, he took this admonition in stride. He laughed and slowed his pace slightly until he had passed the cart and the dog. Then he dropped his hand and allowed his horses to resume the dangerously rapid pace they usually set while traveling the streets of London.

He swung his curricle around the next corner and made his way down Bond Street. He was fast approaching Hookham's Library, when he spotted a very elegant figure of a woman stepping down from a well-appointed barouche in front of one of London's more fashionable shops. The lady was shrouded against the cold, but he had a fairly good notion that he had once again come upon Miss Nerissa Raleigh.

She was dressed in a voluminous cloak of deep blue. The bonnet on her head was trimmed in the same color and fashioned low to cover her ears, hiding most of her shining black curls. As he approached nearer, he still couldn't be certain it was she, but when he saw her suddenly turn back toward the barouche to chatter away in a very animated fashion to a companion who stepped down after her, all remaining doubts fled. It *was* Nerissa.

He had thought often of her since the moment of their meeting the night before, and he was rather glad it was so. The memory of her wide-eyed confidences had proved to offer him a good deal more entertainment than anything he had come across in months.

He didn't think, in all his thirty-one years, he had ever encountered anyone quite like her. She was a strange mixture of innocence and audacity, limpid brown eyes and calculating impulsiveness. Despite her protests and remonstrances, he hadn't believed a word of her nonsense. She was, of a certainty, just another young female with an eye to marrying his fortune and social cache, who no doubt thought she might snare him by appealing to his vanity. The memory of her absurd claims that he might serve as the model for a hero tugged a smile to the corners of his lips.

He had drawn near enough to discern that the woman who accompanied Nerissa bore enough of a resemblance to no doubt be her sister. Together, the ladies entered the shop next door to Hookham's and, on an impulse, he slowed his progress as he approached their carriage.

"Your way is clear," said Henry, thinking his master had adjusted his speed for safety's sake. "You've naught to navigate until the next corner."

"I'm pulling up here. In front of the library, I think."

Henry pulled the muffler away from his ears and bent nearer slightly, the better to catch his master's words. "The—the *library*, Mr. Breck?"

"That's right. I can read, you know," returned his master, one brow flying to a challenging angle.

"Well, of course you can, sir! But—but the *library*? You've never before—"

"Behaved as any other but a frippery fellow? Yes, I know!

And I think it's time I redeemed myself a little in your eyes, don't you?'' asked Breck, turning to survey his tiger's stunned expression with some satisfaction. He waited just long enough for Henry to go to the horses' heads before he tossed him the reins and leapt gracefully down to the shop walk. "As it happens, I'm not interested in the library, but in the shop next door to it. No need to walk them, Henry. I won't be long."

He noticed there were a good number of customers in the shop when he entered. He paused a moment, just inside the door, to tamp the snow from his boots and sweep his hat from his head. The shop patrons turned, and a hushed silence fell over them as they observed his entrance.

He was unperturbed by their scrutiny. Indeed, he was rather used to the fact that his appearance in any quarter was apt to incite a certain level of interest. Too often had he heard himself described as a model of a man of fashion. He wore his brown hair brushed into an artistic arrangement of disorder. His driving coat, which sported no less than fifteen capes, hung from an exquisite pair of shoulders that were the envy of many a man who had tried but failed to emulate his style of dress. He did indeed cut a most impressive figure. He stood a moment, silhouetted against the winter sunlight that shone through the glass-paned door behind him.

Breck cast his gaze about, on the watch for a cloak of deep blue and matching bonnet. He spied her.

Nerissa Raleigh and her sister were on the far side of the store, facing a display of jeweled snuffboxes, their backs toward the door. Of all the patrons in the shop, they alone ignored his presence. They did not turn at his approach, or murmur between them, as the other patrons did, over the stroke of fortune that should find them frequenting the very same shop as Breck Davenant. Instead, their attention remained concentrated on the snuffboxes spread before them.

"This one is very lovely," said Nerissa, indicating a rather large box adorned with a hunting motif.

Anne mentally calculated the cost of the small rubies arranged across the lid of the box. She said in a low voice so none of the other shoppers should overhear, "Oh, but it's very dear. I think if I am to pay such a price for Arthur's gift, I must be assured it will be a gift he shall like above all things."

"Well, why wouldn't he like it?" asked Nerissa reasonably.

Anne hesitated, then said in a faltering voice, "I—I'm not entirely certain he takes snuff, you see."

"Not certain? Anne, you and Arthur have been married almost a year. Do you mean to tell me you still don't know whether your husband takes snuff?" demanded Nerissa in a whispered voice that still conveyed enough incredulity to send the color to her sister's cheeks.

"I suppose we are not very well acquainted, after all," Anne said weakly. "I think I should choose something else for Arthur's Christmas gift."

"But we have looked in almost every shop of fashion in London," said Nerissa with a healthy degree of exaggeration. "If not a snuffbox, then what *will* you give Arthur as a Christmas gift?"

"I—I don't know. But I'm fairly certain I may not give him such a box even if I were sure he took snuff. Goodness, he would scold me blue if he knew the cost of it!"

Nerissa directed her gaze toward the back of the store. Her wide brown eyes scanned the various wares on display, searching for other items that might be suitable for Anne to purchase as a gift for her husband. She spied a familiar face not far away. "Look, Anne. Isn't that Lady Kendrew?"

"It is indeed," said her sister, following her gaze, "and she is with her son, Lord Crompton."

"He's very fine," remarked Nerissa, noting his lordship's stylish mode of dress that stopped just short of dandyism. "Should we speak to them, do you think?"

"Certainly not! We must wait for them to approach us."

"In that case, I rather hope they do not. I don't think I care for Lady Kendrew's coldness. Last night she was not at all a kind and gracious hostess to us."

"I know, dear," said Anne sympathetically, "but for Arthur's sake we must be all politeness no matter how our feelings may be bruised by their treatment."

Lady Kendrew looked up just then from her examination of some table trinkets. Her expression changed dramatically. With a slight wave of her gloved hand she dismissed the shopgirl who had been assisting her, and swept forward on a straight path toward Nerissa and Anne.

"Good heavens, I do believe she is coming in our direction!" Anne exclaimed. "Promise me you shall not do or say anything to jeopardize Arthur's career!"

"As if I would ever do such a thing!" Nerissa replied scornfully.

Lady Kendrew drew nearer, her son following close behind in her majestic wake. As she came abreast of them, Anne nodded in recognition while Nerissa dipped a demure curtsy.

Lady Kendrew and her son ignored them both. Indeed, they sailed regally past, never looking in their direction, their gazes firmly focused upon Breck, who watched their approach with a mordant curl to his lips.

They sailed up to Breck, and Lady Kendrew stretched out both gloved hands in greeting. "My dear nephew! What a surprise to see you here, of all places!"

Breck ignored her left hand but raised the other to his lips in a perfunctory gesture. "Why? Where should I be?" he asked with unnerving directness.

Lady Kendrew tittered gently. "Oh, come! This humble little shop cannot compare at all to the fashionable male haunts you usually frequent, I dare say!"

"That must explain why I find my cousin here, then," he said, acknowledging Lady Kendrew's son with only a lift of his brows. "Enjoying yourself, are you, Crompton?"

Lord Crompton's face flushed slightly, but he replied with a tolerable composure, "As a matter of fact, yes! I was just helping my mother select a gift to give Father for Christmas. I suppose you would consider that sort of thing quite out of your line, Davenant."

"You suppose correctly," replied Breck with infuriating affability. "I never concern myself with such trivial things."

Lord Crompton's color deepened slightly. "I don't consider Christmas a triviality, Davenant," he said challengingly.

"Nor does your cousin Davenant," said Lady Kendrew, stepping into the fast-forming breach. "Can't you see he's merely teasing you, Jamie dear?" She forced a playful, laughing note to her voice and laid a hand on Breck's arm. "Impish Cousin Davenant! You're forever teasing my poor Jamie. Naughty of you too, for you know how my son admires you so!"

"Does he?" asked Breck, casting an appraising eye over his cousin. "I don't see why. I've done nothing admirable."

Lady Kendrew gave another tinkling little laugh. "You *are* a modest one! Never mind, I shan't press you to accept compliments! Tell me instead how your dear brother and sister-in-law go on. Shall we see them at Christmas, do you think?"

"You must ask my brother. *I* could give you arguments for or against them coming here for the holidays, but that would take too long and my horses are standing. Excuse me, won't you? I came in here to see a particular friend of mine."

Without waiting for a reply or reaction, he nodded a farewell and moved on.

He made his way through the other store patrons to where Nerissa and Anne stood, knowing all the while that his aunt and cousin, as well as the other shoppers, were watching with interest. He had seen his aunt snub Nerissa and her sister and had been a good deal taken aback by it. In his lifetime he had come to learn that squelching impertinent mushrooms was a necessary evil, but in his aunt's behavior he had detected a certain ruthlessness that bit a little too near the knuckle. When he had first entered the shop, he had still been toying with the idea of whether to speak to Nerissa. Now, having witnessed Lady Kendrew's incivility, he was possessed with a keen desire to see his aunt served with her own sauce.

Nerissa watched his approach with ever-widening eyes, and when he stood before her and bowed slightly, she could do little more than silently offer her hand in greeting.

"Miss Raleigh. It's a pleasure to see you again," he said.

"When I met you I—I had no idea you were acquainted with Lady Kendrew," she confessed in a rush, mindful of her sister's scolding the night before.

"She's my aunt, actually," said Breck, tossing a negligent glance over his shoulder to where Lady Kendrew and Lord Crompton remained riveted to the spot he had left them by the front door. "How else do you think I came to be invited to last night's affair?"

The memory of Mr. Davenant's treatment at the reception came back to Nerissa in a rush. All his coldness, all his insults, she might have borne very well. But she now perceived, as he looked down upon her, that his expression was a bit too knowing, too mocking for her to believe he was being polite to make amends for his previous behavior.

There was a glint to his gray eyes that was somehow provoking. When he raised one brow and offered her a most charming smile, she was sure that be his words ever so polite, he was finding a great deal of amusement at her expense.

He cast a meaningful glance toward Anne. Nerissa said with little good grace, "Anne, this is Mr. Davenant. He—he is the curricle driver we saw yesterday! My sister, Lady Bridgewater."

"Madam, it is a pleasure. Although I feel I know you very well from our first rather informal meeting yesterday morning. I hope I didn't drive too fast for you to keep up?''

Nerissa choked and tried very hard to favor him with a quelling look. She might have saved herself the trouble, she decided, for he offered back a brief smile that was at once charming and wholly provoking.

So the wretched man had followed them into the store merely for the purpose of teasing them! Nerissa felt her temper rise slightly, at the same time realizing that some of the other store patrons had moved alarmingly close.

She cast a nervous glance about and said in an urgent tone, "Do lower your voice! Heavens, will you not be satisfied until you have told the entire city of London that we followed you yesterday?''

"I assure you," he said with an unwavering gaze, "I would just as soon we kept your behavior our little secret.''

Nerissa wasn't sure what exactly he meant by such words, but she was sure she didn't care to be laughed at. Her full, soft lips pressed into a line of resentment, and she fixed Davenant with a hard stare that her sister recognized immediately.

"We were shopping for a gift to give my husband at Christmas," said Anne, drawing Mr. Davenant's attention away from her Nerissa's sudden mulish silence. "Perhaps you are acquainted with him a little?''

"I'm sure we've met," he replied with a mild disregard for the truth. He saw from Anne's expression that more was required of him, and he dredged up a hazy and long-forgotten vision of a young man too old for his years and too serious by half. "Isn't he the chap who sits on the Treasury Bench?''

Anne smiled. "Yes, that's Arthur. Then you *do* know him! I should like to give him a small gift for Christmas, but I am at a loss to know what. Tell me, Mr. Davenant, what do *you* think would make for suitable gift?''

"I cannot advise you. Although I think I saw some snuff-boxes just behind you.''

Nerissa cast him a look of reproach. "Once again you're being of no help at all. It so happens we aren't even sure Arthur *takes* snuff."

Breck cast a curious glance toward Anne and saw her blush rosily. "Arthur and I have not been married long," she said uncomfortably.

"No matter. Get him something else, then. What would he like most, do you think?"

A heartfelt sigh escaped Anne's lips. "He probably wants more than anything to have one of his horrid bills passed in the Lords."

"I dare say you shall have a deuce of a time giving him *that*. What about you, Miss Raleigh?" he asked, turning toward Nerissa with a distinct gleam to his gray eyes. "What would you like more than anything for Christmas?"

Once again Nerissa was fixed with the certain notion that he was teasing her. She said with a burning look in his direction and a wealth of meaning, "More than anything, I want to see my book published. And if I do get my wish, I shall have the satisfaction of knowing I accomplished it by myself, with no help from anyone."

Her words went wide of their mark. His eyes took on a somewhat metallic gleam that warned her he was about to make her look ridiculous. He set his hat back on his head and said, "Then I hope you may have your wish. In the event you don't, however, you might apply to my aunt. She's very fashionable and can probably tell you where one shops for heroes nowadays! Ladies, it has been a pleasure."

Anne extended her gloved hand and he took it briefly. "Do call," she said, sweetly oblivious of both the meaning behind Breck's words and to her sister's suddenly flushed countenance. "I know Arthur would like very much to renew his acquaintance with you."

"I doubt it, if he's the chap I think he is," said Breck with disarming honesty. He cast his gaze toward Nerissa and added, "I have no turn for politics—although I have found in the past that political receptions can be very entertaining."

He saw the hot blush mantle Nerissa's cheeks and said in a murmuring voice meant just for her, "Don't eat me but smile prettily when I've gone."

He left the store then, with no more than a passing nod toward his aunt and cousin. No sooner did the door shut upon him than everyone in the store, from shopgirl to patron, turned to look at Nerissa and Anne.

"Why is everyone staring at us?" Nerissa demanded of her sister in a hushed tone.

Anne was no more comfortable finding herself the object of such attention than Nerissa was. "I don't know, but Lady Kendrew is looking right at us!"

She was also moving toward them with surprising speed. She came upon them with both hands outstretched, and said in gushing accents, "My dear Lady Bridgewater! And Miss Raleigh! How delightful! I didn't see you there in the corner, or certainly I would have spoken. You know my son, of course!"

Lord Crompton bowed and shook hands, saying, "We met last night, you know. Shouldn't wonder if you don't remember me from all the other guests. Mother's receptions are always shocking squeezes!"

"We—we were very pleased to have been invited," said Anne, a good deal overcome by their sudden attention.

Lady Kendrew surprised them further. "Are you accepting visitors, Lady Bridgewater?" she asked. "Excellent! You must allow my son and me to call, but you must not count on Kendrew! He has no turn for morning calls, I assure you! And I think I shall bring a friend with me. Depend upon us tomorrow morning!"

They were joined then by another lady of fashion who happened to be in the shop to witness Nerissa and Anne in conversation with Breck Davenant. Then they were joined by yet another. Before the sisters at last said their good-byes and left the shop, Lady Kendrew had taken it upon herself to introduce them to all the patrons in the store who were fortunate enough to fall within her ken.

Anne, visibly dazzled by the sudden attention, shook hands very prettily all around, and Nerissa had no choice but to follow suit. But in the back of her mind she knew herself to be making small, polite talk with a clutch of ladies who moments before had not deigned to recognize her.

Nerissa held little doubt that Breck Davenant was the cause behind the crowd of well-wishers surrounding them. For one unnerving moment she entertained the notion that he had known very well that speaking to them would somehow bring them into style.

She wasn't sure whether to be pleased or vexed by the realization, but of one thing she was certain: the more Nerissa learned about Breck Davenant, the more she was convinced that he was indeed the very patterncard of a true romantic hero.

Chapter 6

"I think he knew it," said Nerissa in an emphatic tone the very next afternoon. She and Anne had just finished saying good-bye to the last of a gratifyingly long line of fashionably high-nose callers who, long before Nerissa's arrival in London, had never before exchanged any more than a polite bow with Anne. "I think he was very well aware that his speaking to us would bring us instantly into style."

"You may be right," said Anne. "Lady Kendrew certainly changed once Mr. Davenant left us. And when she and Lady Willingham visited this morning, I was quite in a whirl! Lady Willingham has never spoken to me before. It was very good of her to visit, you know! Such condescension! So very gratifying!"

"So very puzzling," amended Nerissa. "I find it very odd that one man can hold so much influence. And it's even odder that the man should be Breck Davenant! Truly, he has nothing to recommend him. He holds no title, and he cares nothing for fashion or society. Why, then, should it be that he holds such sway over everyone?"

"I'm not sure," said Anne, having given the matter some thought. "But you were certainly quite in his thrall, or we wouldn't have chased him about Piccadilly as we did! *You* thought he was the perfect embodiment of a true romantic hero!"

"Because he was dashing and elegant," said Nerissa. "But now that I have made his acquaintance, I don't know what to think. One moment he is polite and quite pleasant; in the next he is one of the most horrid men I have ever met."

Anne looked at her in mild surprise. "I thought he was charming. And I thought it was very sweet of him to try to claim an acquaintance with Arthur. After all, you and I both know Arthur would no more befriend a man like Mr. Davenant than he would the man in the moon."

"He wasn't sweet to *me*," countered Nerissa throbbingly. "In fact, he treated me rather abominably! He laughed at me and—and threatened to do me physical violence."

Anne regarded her with an expression of patent amusement. "You're exaggerating!"

"I'm not! He threatened to drag me back into the reception hall if I didn't tell him why I was following him. Now, what, I ask, do you call that?"

"Very herolike behavior," said Anne reasonably.

Nerissa sank slowly down onto a chair drawn near the fire. She hated to admit it, but her sister was right. She let loose a slow, rather dramatic sigh and said somewhat reluctantly, "You are right, of course. In my novel, Count du Laney would have said the exact same thing to Lady Hester. Oh, Anne! Was anything ever more provoking? Breck Davenant is perfect! Everything about him is just as Count du Laney should be! His clothes, his walk, his manner of speaking—everything! And now I find that he has merely to crook his finger and the very cream of society bends to his will!"

Anne claimed the chair opposite hers and leaned forward to give her hand a comforting squeeze. "Why don't you ask him again?"

"Because he shall say no again! And if he were to look at me once more with that horridly smug light in his eyes, I couldn't bear it. It's a hard thing, Anne, to have someone laugh at one's dream, I can tell you!" she said in tragic accents.

"I think you are exaggerating," Anne said again, but her tone was gentler this time. "He was so charming to us yesterday, I think he might be a bit regretful that his first meeting with you was less than civil. Ask him again for his help—or, at the very least, think about it!"

But that was part of the trouble, Nerissa realized, for she did think of Breck Davenant—quite often. Everything about him—his dress, his demeanor, his polished air, his assured disregard for the opinions of other—all combined to make Breck Davenant the most compelling man she had ever met.

He was also disagreeably adamant that he would not help her in fashioning the hero for her book. She could not, in all honesty, understand why he would be so reluctant to perform such a simple task.

Anne patted her hand consolingly. "Go to your desk and write to him. With your talent for putting words together, you might be able to persuade him to help you." She left, then, to go upstairs and rest before dressing for the evening; and Nerissa, with little enthusiasm, obediently went to her desk.

Her sister and brother-in-law had very generously allotted to her the table in one corner of the drawing room so Nerissa could continue writing stories while she was in London. On the tabletop, in a very neat stack tied with string, was her manuscript. She hadn't touched it since she had retrieved it from Mr. Heble, the publisher, and she wasn't sure she wanted to touch it now. Then she had a sudden thought.

Breck Davenant was, after all, no longer a total stranger

to her. She reasoned, therefore, that she could probably use what knowledge she had gained of him to achieve her ends. Maybe she didn't need Breck Davenant's help after all; maybe all she needed to do was incorporate into her story the herolike behavior she had already observed about him.

She sat down at the writing desk, untied the string, and set to work, listing all the ways her hero in the piece could be revised to more closely emulate Breck's heroic style and manners. She made a note to change the color of her hero's eyes to gray so they could take on a rather metallic gleam whenever he was about to torment the heroine. She drafted a few sentences that illustrated her hero's ability to quash encroaching mushrooms with a single haughty glance.

Nerissa had reason to be somewhat satisfied with her afternoon's work when at last she climbed the stairs to dress for the evening. She was to accompany Arthur and Anne to a dinner party in the home of Lady Willingham, where, Anne had hinted, there was every possibility for dancing later in the evening.

Nerissa was glad of it. So far, her social schedule since arriving in London had been far from full. In truth, polite society was terribly thin during the winter months, but Nerissa had reason to suspect that her brother-in-law's political leanings, coupled with Lord and Lady Kendrew's prior unwillingness to recognize them, had played a large part in determining their very limited social value.

But no more. Lady Willingham was one of the ladies who, along with Lady Kendrew, had called upon Nerissa and Anne that morning. She was a kindly-looking woman of ample proportions who expressed delight in making the acquaintance at last of two young ladies she had long admired from afar. Lady Willingham had punctuated that very gratifying speech by sweetly handing Anne an invitation to her dinner party that evening along with a heartfelt apology for its lateness.

"Of course, I shouldn't wonder if you were to tell me that your evening is quite full already," she said quite earnestly, "and I can only apologize once again for the stupid error my secretary made in losing your invitation in the first place! But do try to come, dear Lady Bridgewater, won't you?"

Anne, quite easily charmed into taking these words at their face value, assured Lady Willingham that she could count on their attendance. Nerissa was inclined to be a bit suspicious that she and her sister and brother-in-law should suddenly find themselves so much in fashion, but the prospect of actually dancing for the first time in London society held a lure for her too strong to be denied.

They arrived at Lady Willingham's town house at the appointed hour and entered the drawing room, where the guests were to assemble before dinner.

Their hostess uttered a gracious greeting toward Arthur and Anne, then turned her attention toward Nerissa. "Very pretty," she commended, noting Nerissa's gown of orchid watered silk. "Modest but fashionable. Quite befitting a girl on her first tour of London! You will take the *ton* by storm, once the Season starts, I predict! Do come in and meet everyone. You know Lord and Lady Kendrew, of course."

Lady Kendrew came forward immediately to claim Anne's attention. "My dear Lady Bridgewater!" she said effusively as her husband shook hands with Arthur in a rigidly cordial fashion. "Come and sit by me, won't you?"

With Anne and Arthur occupied, Lady Willingham drew Nerissa over to where Lord Crompton was in conversation with a young lady of Nerissa's age.

"Ah, Miss Raleigh! A pleasure to see you again. Let me present Miss Farnham to you," said his lordship with perfect civility. "You have the pleasure, Miss Farnham, of being introduced to Miss Raleigh. I mentioned, I think, that Miss Raleigh is a particular friend of my cousin Davenant."

"That's not true," said Nerissa quickly. She realized her words had been a bit too hasty, and said in a gentler tone, "Mr. Davenant and I are a little acquainted, but I would not presume to claim a friendship with him."

"Very nicely said," commended Lady Willingham. "Many young girls with lesser connections than yours might have been forgiven a prideful reply."

"But—but I have no connection to Mr. Davenant at all!" said Nerissa, determined to clear the air.

"A girl with modesty! How refreshing!" remarked Lady Willingham. "You forget I was there in the shop to see you in conversation with Davenant. I even saw him smile once or twice in your direction!"

Miss Farnham regarded Nerissa with an admiring look. "You travel in exalted circles, Miss Raleigh! Dare I ask if Mr. Davenant will be here tonight?"

"Heavens, how would I know?" asked Nerissa irrepressibly.

Lady Willingham took one of Nerissa's hands in hers and held it fast. "I am relying upon his appearance! In fact, I particularly mentioned in his invitation that you and your sister would be here tonight, my dear. It would be such a treat if he were to show, you know. It's been a good length of time since any hostess was able to rely on Mr. Davenant's attending a party or rout. And even if he were to arrive, he rarely dances or makes the least push to join a conversation. Still," she added with a rather heartfelt sigh, "it would be such a coup if he were to stop in for just a bit!"

Lady Willingham was to have her wish. She was just about to instruct her butler to remove one place setting and do his level best with the tattered remains of her carefully planned seating arrangement, when the door to the drawing room opened and Breck Davenant joined them.

No one was more surprised than she to see him standing there, dressed with impeccable taste and looking the very image of a man of fashion, but she recovered quite nicely.

Lady Willingham swept forward and greeted him with tolerable composure. There was no mistaking the look of triumph to her expression when she handed him around the room, introducing him to one guest after another.

Lord Crompton joined his mother just before they went in to dinner, saying in a tone of mild surprise, "Egad, what maggot has Davenant got into his head this time? This is the first I've seen of my cousin attending a party such as this!"

"He has a very good reason for being here, I dare say," said his mother, shrewdly watching Breck as he patiently submitted to the ministrations of his hostess.

"No, he doesn't," insisted his lordship. "He doesn't attend small parties, for one thing, and I don't believe he has ever set foot in Lady Willingham's house before in his life!"

Lady Kendrew watched Breck greet the Bridgewater party with, she observed keenly, a bit more civility than he had bestowed upon the other guests. He bent over first Nerissa's hand, then Anne's, and favored both ladies with one of his rare smiles. It wasn't hard for her to form a fairly good opinion of the reason behind her nephew's uncommon behavior. But when she saw the manner in which Anne Bridgewater smiled back up at him, her opinion quickly turned to something a little more absolute. "Jamie, almost I wash my hands of you!" she said with a small flash of impatience.

Since dinner was at that moment announced, Lord Crompton was given a reprieve from seeing his mother do just so. He had instead the satisfaction of escorting Nerissa Raleigh in to dinner.

Nerissa was glad to be paired with him, for she had been given an opportunity to get to know Lord Crompton a little better and had come to revise her initial opinion of him. Since their first meeting, when his demeanor had been less than friendly, she had come to realize that he was a most amiable young man. He was handsome too, for he had inherited the Davenant good looks, but she thought he lacked the force of character and innate sense of style that distinguished his cousin, Breck.

Throughout their meal, Lord Crompton proved to be an attentive dinner partner. Still, Nerissa couldn't prevent her gaze from wandering from time to time toward the head of the table, where Breck sat at the right hand of their hostess. Inevitably, her conversation with Lord Crompton followed where her eyes had strayed.

She chanced to compliment his lordship upon the design of his waistcoat, and he immediately credited Breck Davenant with its creation.

"My cousin is a dashed respected leader of fashion, you know."

"He is certainly in fine looks tonight," she agreed.

"Style comes naturally to him, I think," said Lord Crompton, studying his cousin at the far end of the table. "You don't see shoulders like that on many men. And he's an uncommon bruiser, for all his grace."

Nerissa frowned. "A bruiser? What is that?"

"A boxer! A man handy with his fives!"

"Are you telling me that Mr. Davenant has been in— in *fights*?"

"Not fights—brawls!" his lordship corrected Nerissa. "I've seen him in action. He came to my rescue once when I set up a fellow's hackles at a race meeting. I didn't mean to insult the man, of course, and the whole thing was a great misunderstanding. But my cousin Davenant stepped right in—right between three fellows and me—and appeared for all the world as if he would take the lead in the mill—and would enjoy very much doing them all in!"

Nerissa regarded him with wide eyes. "Gracious! What happened?"

"It all came to nothing. One look in those eyes of his and a charging elephant would have backed off."

"He's very brave," she said appreciatively. "How fearless he was to have stepped in to save you so!"

"Oh, I don't think he did it to save me. I think he was merely in the mood to char someone's roast, and that presented as good an opportunity as any."

Nerissa digested this bit of information and decided that there was more to Mr. Breck Davenant than she could ever have guessed. She resolved to learn more, and asked hopefully, "Is he a Corinthian?"

Lord Crompton considered the question. "I don't think so, for he holds himself too much apart to join that set. But now that I come to think on it, he is something of a sword master and he's deadly with a pistol."

Nerissa mentally added these achievements to an already burgeoning list of Mr. Davenant's very herolike accomplishments.

After dinner the guests assembled in the gallery, where dancing was to be got up. The music started and Nerissa was led out to the dance floor by Lord Crompton.

She walked out on his arm and took her place in the country set with a good deal of evident happiness. At last she was to dance in London! She put out of her mind the tedious reception she had been forced to endure at Lady Kendrew's house and thought instead of how entertaining the coming evening promised to be.

She had just gone down the first row of a country dance, when a change in the direction of her steps caused her to turn and look at the far side of the room, where Breck was standing. He was with a small group of men, all speaking and laughing jovially about him. His pose was unconcerned, but his eyes were on her, his expression somewhat speculative. She turned away and concentrated on her dance steps. When she next chanced to spot him, he had left the clutch of bucks and was making his way about the perimeter of the dance floor to where Anne and Arthur were standing.

"Mr. Davenant!" said Anne very kindly. "Do let me reacquaint you with my husband!"

Breck sketched a polite bow and taxed his fleeting memory. "I think we've met before, haven't we? Last Season—a bout at Fives Court, wasn't it?"

"That's right," said Arthur. "You gave me a devil of a dressing-down that night, if you'll recall."

"Did I? To tell you the truth, I *don't* recall, but my apologies all the same. Tell me, I didn't have you on toast, did I?"

"Very nearly!" responded Arthur with a smile. "It was pretty justified, I can say now, although when it happened, I felt very sorely used indeed!"

"Forgive me!" Breck said in a voice of simple sincerity that he hoped would mask the fact that aside from what he had already divulged, he had no other memory of that day.

"It is I who should apologize," said Arthur candidly. "Last summer I had just been appointed to the Treasury and was about to take Anne as my wife. I was pretty puffed up, I can tell you, and doing a lot of talking just to hear myself speak, if you know what I mean. I was at Fives Court with a friend. I spotted Lord Kendrew and immediately tried to buttonhole him with talk of a bill I wanted to see passed in the Lords. You were standing nearby. Apparently, my incessant prattling about corn prices put you on your ear, and probably deservedly so. You threatened to throw me out of the place."

"It sounds very much like something I would say. I don't usually tolerate mixing business with pleasure—especially when the pleasure is a fisticuffs bout.

"That's where we differ, I suppose. You see, I wouldn't have been there in the first place had my friend not insisted I accompany him. I assure you, I usually find better ways to fill my time than watching two men pummel the life from each other."

"Do you?" asked Breck, looking down upon him with his brows slightly raised. "Another difference between us: you, I gather, are a man of great scruples, while I haven't any scruples at all."

"I beg your pardon! I didn't mean that the way it sounded," said Arthur, a stricken expression on his face. "I suppose I can be a bit too single-minded, but that's only because I consider my work in the Lords to be of the utmost importance!"

"I don't doubt for a moment that it is," said Breck with a slight, discomfiting smile that rarely failed to end a conversation. "Someday you must tell me what the devil is discussed in the House of Lords that can incite so much dedication."

Arthur divined most correctly that this was not the day Mr. Davenant had in mind. "I—it doesn't appear that you and I have much in common," he said.

They fell to silence and contented themselves with watching the dancers. Once again Breck's gaze settled on Nerissa.

She knew he was watching her, and she felt her dance steps falter a bit. From the moment he had entered the ballroom, Nerissa was deeply aware that his regard had been almost constant. It wasn't that his gaze was in any way penetrating or disturbing, but for some reason she felt a little unsure whenever she perceived that his eyes were upon her. She wished he would look away; she wished he would leave her sister's side and direct his attentions toward some other guest in the ballroom, but her wishes came to naught and his gaze continued to follow her.

She wasn't the only one to have noticed that Breck Davenant had singled out the Bridgewater party for a good portion of his attentions. Lady Kendrew had been studying his movements since he arrived, and she wasn't at all sure she liked what she saw.

When her son came to stand at her side, she said in her most stately manner, "It is a pity your cousin Davenant should take such a quirkish interest in the Bridgewaters. I assure you, I shouldn't deign to recognize them otherwise!"

Lord Crompton frowned slightly. "They're a harmless

family, I think. Bridgewater himself is a bit stolid for my taste, but his wife and sister-in-law are charming, I think."

"You are mistaken," said his mother with majestic calm. "Neither girl has anything to recommend her to our circle of friends."

"They've certainly captured Davenant's attention!"

"Exactly! And if I know my nephew—and I do!—I would be tempted to think he has found another flirt."

Lord Crompton frowned. "Davenant? I shouldn't think so! He's just taken up with Lady Sodington again. He's been constant with her since your reception the other night."

"Oh, he has not cast Lady Sodington aside, I assure you! No, indeed! But it does appear he has merely found another to add to his list of conquests."

Lord Crompton's frown increased. "The Raleigh chit? Pshaw! He don't nod twice at green girls! Why, Davenant would as lief flirt with a cat!"

"I don't mean the younger one, Jamie dear. She's much too wide-eyed and innocent for his tastes. I'm speaking, instead, of the elder one. The Bridgewater *woman.*"

Lord Crompton put up his quizzing glass and surveyed Anne speculatively. "Do you think? I had a chance to speak to her before, and I didn't find her much more sophisticated than the younger sister! I don't think she is at all the sort of woman Davenant would set his sails for!"

"Exactly!" said his mother knowingly. "It would be just like your cousin Davenant to do the very opposite of what everyone *thinks* he will do! Only consider! She's pretty enough, and she has a very pliant nature. Even more important, she doesn't seem the type to gossip or speak out of turn, and you know Davenant likes his women to fly close!"

Lord Crompton considered this bit of logic. "Egad, you may be right! He did make a point of speaking to her in the Bond Street shop."

"And the Bridgewater woman was well aware of the honor, if you ask me!"

"I dare say she was charmed by him! He can be very obliging when he wants to be."

His mother flicked an impatient glance over him. "You are just as charming, my dear Jamie," she said. "More is the pity that you should always find yourself coming in second to your cousin Davenant."

Lord Crompton colored a bit. "I don't dwell on comparisons between my cousin and me, you know. I should drive myself to distraction otherwise!"

"There should be no comparison, to begin with," uttered her ladyship. "You are just as stunning an object of admiration as Breck Davenant—more so when one considers your title and fortune! Yet, it is your cousin who leads society and forces us to follow where he goes. If it were not for a freakish whim that drives him to bring the Bridgewaters into style, I assure you, I never would have recognized them!"

"They're not so very far beneath our touch," said Lord Crompton, feeling some defense was necessary.

"Then you forget all the backhanded turns Lord Bridgewater has dealt your father in the Lords. I could never forgive such behavior! You may dispense your loyalties where you see fit!"

His lordship was well aware that there was no good to come from arguing with his mother when she adopted that majestic tone. That her nose had always been a bit out of joint in regard to Breck Davenant he had long been aware, and while Lord Crompton had never been one to begrudge his cousin's social status, he knew very well that his mother considered Breck's notoriety to be nothing less than some freakish mishap. She had long been jealous of her nephew and had long believed quite fervently that society's admiration and accolades were being heaped upon the wrong young man.

"I cannot help but wonder," she said with regal calm,

"what the marchioness would say if she knew her young brother-in-law had chosen to take up with an unsuitable young woman."

Lord Crompton looked doubtful. "Lady Bridgewater is not really so very unsuitable, is she?"

"Of course she is! Her mother is a fool and her sisters all married stupid husbands! Not one of them is accepted in the better homes of the Five Hundred!"

"You're not thinking of writing to the marchioness again, are you?" asked Lord Crompton. "You were made to suffer the last time you wrote her to complain of Davenant's behavior."

"It is my duty to keep the head of the House of Davenant aware of what goes on within the family. I think the marchioness would be very interested to know that Breck Davenant has given himself over to some rather aberrant behavior. Don't worry that I shall be at all indiscreet," she added, noting the doubtful frown on her son's brow. "But do know that I have only the family's best interest at heart!"

Chapter 7

It was two evenings later when next Nerissa saw Breck Davenant. She and her sister and brother-in-law had been invited to a small party of music and cards. The evening was half over before Breck arrived, and Nerissa, seated on a rout chair between Anne and their new friend, Miss Farnham, chanced a look over her shoulder in time to see him shaking hands most cordially with their hostess.

"Heavens! Breck Davenant is here," she hissed.

Miss Farnham's eyes lit. "Is he? If only he would speak to us for just a moment, I should consider this the perfect evening!"

Nerissa wasn't at all sure she wanted to fall under his notice again. From the moment he had teased her in the Bond Street shop, she had been quite fearful that he might say something that would betray the fact that she had behaved rashly and imprudently by following him in the streets. Since the first time Nerissa had mentioned Breck Davenant's name, Anne had never missed an opportunity to impress upon her how easily her thoughtless actions might repel Mr. Davenant and thus hurt Arthur's career and Anne's social status. Every time she saw Breck move in her direction or felt his eyes upon her, she was half afraid he meant to tease her over her behavior. If, by chance, he spoke too loud while doing so, or if someone were to overhear, Nerissa knew the results might be disastrous.

"I for one hope he never speaks to us again," said Nerissa, willing him to stay away.

"Rissa! How can you say such a thing?" demanded Anne. "Why, Mr. Davenant has been kindness itself to us."

Miss Farnham added helpfully, "And he was very cordial when I was introduced to him at Lady Willingham's party. He even shook my hand!"

"From all I have heard, Mr. Davenant's kindness is more an exception than rule," said Nerissa.

"I overheard my mother speaking of him once," said Miss Farnham, "and she said he was nothing but a rascal!"

"Goodness! Is your mother acquainted with Mr. Davenant?" asked Anne.

"No, but she is a little acquainted with Lady Kendrew, who is a severe critic of Mr. Davenant's. I didn't intend to overhear their conversation, you understand, but I was merely in the next room and the door *was* open. . . ."

"Only tell us what Lady Kendrew said to your mother!" demanded Nerissa. "Was it very bad? Is he very evil?"

"Not evil precisely," said Miss Farnham. "Mr. Davenant is the youngest of eleven brothers and sisters, and Lady Kendrew said he has been spoilt and petted since the day he was born. She said his oldest brother, the marquess, and his wife are quite to blame as much as his parents, for they continue to indulge him. And I understand his fortune is so great because he swindled his grandmother, the old duchess, into leaving all her riches to him!"

"He *does* sound like a rascal!" said Nerissa, her interest piqued. "What else did your mama and Lady Kendrew say about him? Is he a seducer of women? Has he any dark secrets?"

Anne clutched her hand in a forbidding grip. "I rather think you're letting your imagination run away with you, Rissa, and I hope you shall not speak of such things when next you meet Mr. Davenant."

Since she had gone almost the entire evening at Lady Willingham's dinner party without speaking more than a few words to him, Nerissa didn't think there was much of a chance Breck Davenant would pursue an acquaintance with her. In fact, she rather hoped he would not, for she didn't think she would care to suffer through another round of his horrid teasing about heroes and gothic romance novels.

Such hopes were quickly vanquished. She looked up to see Breck Davenant striding straight toward her. Alarmed by the thought of meeting him again, she jumped quickly to her feet.

Anne followed suit, saying, "Be nice to him, Rissa, please! And promise me you won't say anything to upset him! We owe him so much already!"

Nerissa didn't think she wanted to be any more beholden to a man who could laugh at her as easily as Breck seemed to be able to do. She watched him move inexorably toward her through the sea of guests, and felt very much like a lamb waiting for a wolf to pounce. She decided that however much her sister wanted her to stay, she couldn't abide standing by to suffer another round of his teasing.

Before Anne or Miss Farnham could stop her, she slipped away to a small alcove set with potted ferns and tall palms. It looked a rather inviting and likely place for her to spend a few moments until she was sure Mr. Davenant had moved on to other guests, away from her sister's side.

It never occurred to Nerissa that he would follow her, but that was exactly what he did. He made his way through the crowd, past Anne and Miss Farnham, on a direct course toward Nerissa. For a brief, ill-judged moment she thought to hide from him and ducked behind one of the potted palms. Further reflection told her that the long, thin fronds could never hide her completely from his view. If he were to come upon her, half hidden behind the plants, she would appear nothing short of ridiculous.

She stepped back out from behind the palm, resolved to stand and face him if he chose to speak to her, but she was unable to move very far. One of the horrid, featherlike leaves was caught in the ornament in her hair.

For the briefest of moments she considered engaging in a very undignified struggle with the palm frond. But as she saw, with no small amount of alarm, that Mr. Davenant was very close upon her, she decided instead to stand very still where she was and hope that he wouldn't notice her predicament.

With any luck, he would speak to her only briefly and would move on without realizing that the abominable plant held her captive.

"I thought I might find you in this direction," said Breck, eyeing with interest the absurdly regal angle in which she was holding her head. "The music has started. May I have the honor, Miss Raleigh?"

Nerissa felt her heart thud against her ribs and silently cursed the cloying palm frond. How much she wanted to dance—and how much she would like to be partnered by such a heroic man as Breck Davenant! But she couldn't very well do so while joined at the head to an oversized pot of greenery.

"Would—would you mind very much if we *didn't* dance?" she asked.

"Not at all. We'll share instead a nice, long chat."

This time the subject of Nerissa's silent cursings included Breck Davenant. She wished with all her might that he would leave.

He remained, however, steadfastly by her side. He looked down upon her and noticed, most appreciatively, the manner in which the pale pink color of her dress complimented the subtle blush of her cheeks. Her shining black hair was caught up on top of her head in a swirl of curls into which a slim ornament of pearls had been set.

She was in excellent looks, and since he was a man who did not often meet with a rebuff when he favored an attractive lady with his attentions, he was a little intrigued that she should have refused his invitation to dance.

He said, a teasing note in his voice, "Have you discovered here tonight any gentlemen worthy of being followed? I dare say there are any number of men present who might timber up to a hero's weight!"

Although he had spoken softly so only she might hear, Nerissa, her hair still trapped by the potted palm, cast her wide brown eyes swiftly about, fearful lest any of the other guests might have overheard.

"No!" she said adamantly. "There is only one man to whom I have ever ascribed the qualities of a hero—and I very much regret having done so, I assure you!"

He smiled then, greatly amused. "Never say so, or I shall begin to think I have sunk greatly in your esteem."

"If you have a mind to tease me, sir, I beg you to move on!" she said in a tone that was just as rigid as the angle at which she was being forced to hold her head.

"All right. I'll be sensible. Shall I start by losing your curls from that palm frond?" he asked with a pointed look that convinced her he had known all along about her predicament.

Her eyes widened for the barest of moments. "Do you mean you knew? Even when you asked me to dance, you knew?"

"Forgive me," he said simply. "It was cruel of me, but I think that's why I enjoyed it so much."

There was no use in pretending she wasn't in a fix. She said with growing warmth in her cheeks, "If you would be so good!"

He laughed softly. "Hold still and try to appear as if nothing is amiss. Let's see if we can't have you free before anyone else notices, shall we?"

He applied his nimble fingers to the task and had her loose in an instant.

"Thank you!" she said, patting the newly liberated curl back into place. "I can't begin to tell you how embarrassing that was. You quite saved me!"

"Think nothing of it, Miss Raleigh. We heroes do that sort of thing every day."

He was smiling again, that infuriatingly mocking smile that Nerissa had come to notice a bit too often for her own comfort. "There are few things in life I regret," she said, "but confiding that you were a model hero is one of them!"

He laughed, very much amused at this revelation. "Does that mean I have succeeded in revising your opinion of me?"

"Is that what you *want* to do?" she asked, surprised. "Do you want to warn me off? Do you think that by teasing me and making me feel foolish you shall convince me that you are not the stuff of heroes after all?"

"Perhaps. It's a pity to disappoint you, but you may as well learn at last, Miss Raleigh, what all the rest of society has known about me for years."

"I may be young, but I am an excellent judge of character, I assure you," she said with confidence. "You shall never be able to convince me you are less than heroic."

"I see. In your experience, would a hero, such as you imagine me to be, attend a musical party as this one?" he asked.

She gave the matter some thought before replying. "I cannot say for certain, but I think this evening might prove a bit insipid for a true hero. I should rather think the hero in the kind of book I write would be more at home at his club, blowing a cloud with his friends and enjoying a drink over a turn of the cards."

"Then a hero I must be, for what you just described is exactly what I intend to do." He took her hand and bowed slightly over it. "Good evening, Miss Raleigh. As always, it has been a pleasure."

He was gone before she could say another word. She watched him move through the crowd of guests with the same swashbuckling grace that had first captured her attention. Other guests followed his movement as well, and some of the lucky ones received a touch on the shoulder or a shake of the hand as he passed them on his way to the door.

Nerissa's heart swelled as she realized the effect his presence was having on the assembly. Freakish humors he may have, and a horrid tease he may be, but watching Mr. Breck Davenant move the through crowd only seemed to convince Nerissa that he was, in fact, as close to a true, living, breathing hero as any man she could ever hope to meet.

Chapter 8

The Christmas Ball at the German Embassy was, Anne assured her sister, the highlight of the holiday season. "Simply anyone who is anyone attends!" she added with all the authority of one who had come to consider herself among that select group.

"I hope Mr. Davenant is not *anyone*," said Nerissa passionately, and incurred a sharp look from her sister.

They were seated in the drawing room, waiting for Arthur to join them before they set off for the embassy, and Anne felt compelled to offer her sister a piece of advice. "You may not be aware, Rissa dear, but I have come to realize that we owe every bit of our success to Mr. Davenant! Since the moment he spoke to us in the shop on Bond Street, all the parties, all the balls, every entertainment offered us—we owe them all to Mr. Davenant!"

To Mr. Davenant, Nerissa also owed her rescue from a potted palm, but she didn't think she wanted tell Anne of it. Nor did she wish to mention the way in which Breck Davenant seemed to hold all her romantic ideals up to ridicule.

Even more important, she didn't want to tell her sister how often Breck intruded upon her thoughts. As infuriating as he was, as horrid his sense of humor, she truly didn't think there could be another man in England who so epitomized the perfect romantic hero. She admired him as much for his handsome looks as for his dashing and confident air.

Truly, she had never before found herself so undecided and confused. She very much wished to please her sister and encourage Mr. Davenant's attentions; yet she knew that would mean being subjected to his teasings and ridicules. But no matter how much he may laugh at her ideas of heroes and romance, Nerissa was still drawn to him and longed to feel again the warm gaze of his gray eyes on her.

She tried to push all thoughts of Breck Davenant from her mind as she idly traveled the drawing room, waiting for Arthur to join them before they set off for the embassy ball. She was wearing a new gown of white Albany gauze over a slip of white satin. A band of ribbon the color of claret caught her dress just below her bosom, and a slightly thinner ribbon of the same hue was tied in a simple bow about her slender neck. A handful of rosebuds of the same color, fashioned in silk, were woven between the curls of her black hair.

"I hope," said Anne, "you will remember to be on your best behavior if Mr. Davenant speaks to you. If you should run off again, as you did the other night at the musical, I shall faint dead away from shame!"

But Nerissa was destined to repeat her conduct, for no sooner did she arrive with Anne and Arthur at the home of the German ambassador, than she found Breck Davenant already in attendance.

She cast a swift glance at him and he met her gaze evenly. He didn't appear to be laughing at her, or even the least bit amused. She vowed that she wouldn't be made to suffer yet again another serving of his raillery.

She knew from experience that Breck Davenant rarely

stayed long at any assembly and often departed within minutes of his arrival. Surely, in the vast spaces of the German Embassy, there had to be a place Nerissa could hide. If she could find a room, a safe retreat, she thought, she could wait until he quit the ball and she would not have to face him.

Lord Crompton was the first guest to approach them. He bowed toward Arthur and said, "Good evening! Miss Raleigh! Lady Bridgewater! How lovely you both look! Surely you are the prettiest girls here tonight!"

Anne blushed rosily. "That's quite the nicest compliment I have received in some time."

"Then say you'll thank me by giving me the favor of the first dance. You don't mind, do you, Bridgewater?"

"Oh, Arthur never dances," said Anne before Arthur could respond. She placed her hand on his arm and said, "I should love to be your partner for this and any other dance you care to name!"

Arthur watched them take their places in the set and muttered, "I *do* dance—I just never realized that Anne cared so much for it!"

"I'll dance with you, Arthur," said Nerissa helpfully.

He looked down at her as if noticing her presence for the first time. "No, no! You shall have all the bucks in line to partner you. You don't need me cutting in their line. I—I think I'll just wait here for Anne," he said, his eyes following her every movement as she moved across the floor on Lord Crompton's arm.

With Anne dancing and Arthur occupied, Nerissa found that it was a relatively easy thing to slip away and avoid Breck's presence. The ballroom was crowded indeed, and a crush of elegantly dressed guests masked her movements as she went back into the great hall and climbed the staircase to the next floor.

She thought no one paid the least attention to her, but she reckoned without Breck. He had been watching her since her arrival and he had noticed immediately upon seeing her that she did not at all appear to be herself. He was used to seeing expressions of optimism and buoyancy written across her face. It was, perhaps, her eternal belief in heroes and castles in the air that was part of her charm. But tonight when he had first seen her, and their eyes had met, he had detected a wariness to her expression that he had not seen before.

He watched her leave her sister's side and the ballroom. An impulse sent him after her.

He followed her to the next landing on the stair, off which ran the family apartments. In the distance the music from the ballroom could be heard, and Breck quietly traveled the hallway and opened the first door he found.

He entered a small saloon lit by a fire in the hearth and an oversized candelabrum that stood on a side table. The room was already decorated for Christmas with bowers of holly strung across the mantel and pine boughs hung over the doorways. In the center of the room, standing stock-still, was Nerissa.

"Miss Raleigh, you have a decided penchant for escaping assemblies," he said, that quizzing note in his voice.

He closed the door and advanced farther into the room. It took a moment for him to realize that Nerissa had not replied, nor even turned to look at him. She remained curiously still, her attention focused upon one of the most dazzling objects she had ever beheld.

In the far corner of the room stood a pine tree that reached just above Breck's height. About its branches were hung a number of adornments. Perfectly round oranges, bowed ribbons, and small brass keepsakes decorated the tree from top to bottom. Set among the branches were short candles of purest white, held in place by small sconces of polished brass.

Breck moved toward one corner of the room, the better to see Nerissa's profile as she continued to gaze at the tree, her brown eyes gone wide with wonder.

"Shall I light them for you?" he asked at last in a low voice that was just as mesmerizing as the tree itself.

He didn't wait for her to answer, but drew a taper from the candelabrum and began to light the candles on the tree. Nerissa clasped her hands together and watched him with a feeling of deepening anticipation. When he was done, he stepped back, allowing her a full view of the results.

The candlelight amid the branches seemed to set the entire tree aglow; it reflected off the small brass tokens and bathed the room in the warmth of its beauty.

Nerissa couldn't recall the last time she had been so dazzled. She closed her eyes for just a moment and breathed deeply of the scent of pine and oranges. "Could anything ever be more beautiful?" she asked appreciatively. "It's almost as if a forest nymph had touched the tree with its magical fairy dust! It—it's the most wonderful thing I have ever seen!"

She looked over at Breck and found his gray eyes upon her, his lips half-smiling, and an oddly arrested expression on his face. "I dare say you think me quite foolish!" she said, steeling herself against the teasing she thought surely he would hurl her direction.

He took the time to draw a cigarillo from his vest pocket and light it from the flame of the candelabrum before he answered. "On the contrary," he said slowly, "I think you quite charming."

She felt a sudden and unaccountable wave of happiness sweep over her, and she was somewhat surprised by the feeling. She watched him cross the space between them with a few long-legged strides. He chose not to expand upon those brief, provocative words, electing instead to stand by her side and gaze upon the tree with her in companionable silence.

"Why is it here?" she asked after a few moments.

"It's a Christmas tree. The Germans make them part of their holiday celebrations."

"I—I've never heard of such a thing!" she said, looking up at him and finding the quizzing look had returned to his eyes.

"Barbaric, isn't it?" he asked. "No doubt they erect it as part of a pagan ritual. Do you think they dance like heathens about it and—"

"Don't!" exclaimed Nerissa, laying her small hand on his sleeve to still his words. "Please don't make sport of it. It—it's the most beautiful thing I've ever seen!"

Breck, long inured to the lures of Christmas traditions, even those of German origin, thought better than to tease her over this admission.

He stepped back a little toward the fireplace, drew deeply against his cigarillo, and watched the play of emotions cross her expressive face. It had been a long time since he had seen anyone so lose herself to enchantment. In his social circle, one rarely encountered anything new. If, by odd circumstance, one did, it would never do to betray the thing.

Nerissa Raleigh, he was fast discovering, had no such compunctions. She gave herself up to the delight of her surroundings and gazed upon the softly glowing tree with wide-eyed, unaffected appreciation. He had the very distinct feeling that she didn't even recall the Christmas Ball going on downstairs, or the fact that someone might have by now missed her. Were he to allow it, she would no doubt prefer to remain in the family saloon, staring at the tree for the rest of the evening.

"Miss Raleigh," he said in a quiet voice that drew her attention. "It is time we were returned to the ballroom."

"I suppose you are right," she said, fighting back an odd pang of regret. She watched him move about the tree, extinguishing the candles, and she said rather impulsively, "Thank you! How gallant you were to have lit the candles and made the tree so lovely just for my benefit!"

He had just finished snuffing the last of the flames, and

turned to send one of his quizzing looks her direction. "I dare say I was merely in one of my heroic moods."

She didn't appear to be the least offended. "I dare say you are more often heroic than you may know!"

He looked down upon her, a speculative look in his eye, as if he had been about to say something but thought better of it. Instead, he offered his arm and said rather gently, "I'll take you back now."

Nerissa placed her hand on his arm and felt the warmth fly to her cheeks. Here was a side of Breck Davenant she had not yet seen! He was being extremely solicitous and surprisingly tender. When he led her back into the ballroom and she would have withdrawn her hand from the crook of his arm, he placed his other hand over hers, compelling her to stay.

"Will you dance with me, Miss Raleigh?" he asked.

She could hardly refuse. In fact, at that very moment she wanted nothing more than to remain by his side. They took their place in a country set. The music struck up and Breck clasped her hand lightly. He may as well have set her gloves on fire, thought Nerissa, for each time the movement of the dance set her hand in his, his touch left behind a most peculiar warmth. They had been together many times, but now, inexplicably, she was nervous in his presence and could barely bring herself to meet his eyes without blushing.

Breck noticed her behavior, and he was a little intrigued by it. Her whole demeanor had changed since he had lit the candles on the Christmas tree. He recalled how lovely she had looked—her wide brown eyes gazing upon the tree with an ingenuous light that was not at all unattractive. His impulse had been to tease her, but when she had directed that same gaze his way, he had felt something stir in his heart that was not mere amusement.

He had meant to twit her, but instead found himself feeling something quite tender for her. That, he knew, was dangerous ground.

By the time the country dance came to an end, he had regained the mastery of himself. With the last note of music, he was able to harden himself against those more tender feelings that had taken him by surprise a few moments before.

He led Nerissa back to where Anne and Arthur were standing and bowed over her hand before he released her. "Thank you, Miss Raleigh, for a very enjoyable dance."

He smiled slightly and moved away, remaining in the ballroom just long enough to bid good night to the ambassador and his wife.

Chapter 9

Nerissa and her sister were lingering over their breakfast, when Nerissa let out a long, rather dramatic sigh.

"It hardly feels like Christmas at all," she said rather wanly.

"Perhaps it is because you have had your nose to your work for the past two days," Anne scolded. "I can't imagine you would feel the least bit festive when all you have done is closet yourself in the drawing room and work on your book."

"Working on my book has nothing to say to the matter. Do you realize, Anne, that this year will be the first time I have been away from home for Christmas? I think I'm feeling rather melancholy."

Anne smiled slightly. "What shall it take to erase your melancholy, dear Rissa?"

"We could decorate the house," she replied promptly. "We could put up Christmas boughs just like at home, and set Cook to laying by sweetmeats and biscuits and— oh, and a pudding! We must have a pudding, Anne!"

Her sister laughed. "I don't see why we may not set

Cook to work, and I shall ask Arthur if we may not decorate the little sitting room."

"I'm sure he won't mind," said Nerissa confidently.

"I dare say you are right, as long as the decorations we devise are tasteful and not too overwhelming."

"Once the house is decorated, perhaps Arthur will allow us to have one or two guests in, just to say Happy Christmas!"

"Decorate the house?" repeated Anne. "Rissa dear, you know very well it is bad luck to put up any Christmas ornamentation before Christmas Eve."

"But the German Embassy was decorated," reasoned Nerissa, "and the family apartments were beautifully adorned."

"That's different," said Anne with superiority. "The ambassador and his wife are German, and they may very well hold to their own customs. We, however, are not German, but English, and we shall hold to our own traditions. That means, Rissa dear, that we shall not put up our Christmas bowers or kissing boughs until the day before Christmas."

"But we could gather them now, couldn't we?" pursued Nerissa. "We could go out and collect the pine branches and the holly and mistletoe before times."

"No, we may not. When the time comes to gather the things we shall need to decorate the house, we shall send the servants out."

"It doesn't sound as if it shall prove to be the least bit entertaining!" said Nerissa pessimistically.

"We do not do it because it is entertaining or amusing, Rissa dear. We do it because it is our duty to prepare for Christmas and to share it with our employees."

Nerissa cast her sister a long, appraising look. "Do you know, just now you sounded very much like Arthur."

Anne looked back at her with an expression of dawning horror. "Goodness! I do believe you are right! Oh, Rissa, I did—I *did* just say exactly what Arthur would have said!"

"Anne, you don't suppose you are beginning to think like Arthur, do you? You aren't going to begin speaking of politics and legislation needed to control the price of corn, I hope!"

"I'm just as stunned as you are!" said Anne, deeply shaken. "I suppose I never realized how great an influence Arthur has had over me."

"You could shake off his influence by doing the exact opposite of what you know he would like you to do," suggested Nerissa.

"If you're suggesting that we decorate the house for Christmas, the answer must still be, no, Nerissa. Arthur would not like it above half."

Nerissa didn't intend to let the matter drop. Her head had been filled with thoughts of Christmas trees and kissing boughs since the night of the embassy ball, and she was rather determined to recreate the beauty and enchantment of the ambassador's saloon in the drawing room of Bridgewater House.

She would have found another argument to put forth to convince her sister that the house must be decorated for Christmas with all speed, but the door to the dining room opened and the Bridgewaters' very efficient butler entered.

He announced, in a suitably lowered voice, that there appeared to be some trouble in the main hall.

"Oh, dear," said Anne. "And Arthur has already gone out."

"What kind of trouble, Bellamy? You're not speaking of hooligans or thieves, are you?" asked Nerissa.

"No, miss. That sort of trouble we deal with quite quickly and efficiently, I assure you. No, this is very different. I am sorry to say, miss, but there is a person at the door and he is demanding to be allowed to leave a—a *package* for you!"

"For me?" repeated Nerissa, looking from Bellamy's

worried expression to Anne, who appeared quite alarmed. "What on earth could it be?"

Bellamy cleared his throat and said in the confidential manner of a trusted old retainer, "Judging from the nature of the gift, miss, I don't think the man is possessed of all his senses. Still, he is demanding that the gift be delivered and with the utmost secrecy! He was very insistent that I not tell you about it until after he had left. Frankly, miss, I don't think this particular person would know how many beans make five, but I cannot persuade him to leave!"

"Oh, dear! A Bedlamite!" said Anne worriedly. "I *do* wish Arthur were at home!"

Nerissa gave the matter some thought. Her curiosity, always keen under the most tedious circumstances, was now careening full force. She was quite determined to see for herself the kickup in the main hall and said, "Do you think, Bellamy, I would be in any danger if I were to see the man for myself?"

"Danger, miss? Oh, no! Not with me and two footmen standing by! And the person is not wholly unpresentable, after all, even though his behavior is odd in the extreme!"

"Then I shall see for myself what he's about," she replied, squaring her slim shoulders purposefully.

Bellamy held the door for her, and she sailed past him and down the stairs. Her mien was brave, her expression, when she reached the entry hall, quite regal, and she was able to maintain that pose as long as she could hear the comforting footsteps of Anne and Bellamy following close behind.

As promised, two footmen were standing guard near the front door, and in the center of the hall stood a man almost concealed from head to toe by greenery. He looked up through a veil of pine branches as Nerissa descended the last of the stair. She recognized him at almost the very moment she realized what he was about.

"Why, it's *you!*" she exclaimed, although her attention was fairly riveted on the tall pine tree that threatened to smother him within its branches. "You're Mr. Davenant's tiger! Anne, this man is not at all dangerous! Shame on you, Bellamy, for making him out to be a raving lunatic, when anyone can see he has merely brought us a tree!"

Henry shot the butler a fulminating look. "I told you my master didn't want anyone to know of this business until after I was gone!"

"Don't be angry with Bellamy. I would have known your master was responsible for such a lovely gesture even had you escaped without my seeing you!" said Nerissa, quite starry-eyed.

"What," demanded Anne, "do you mean, he has brought us a tree?"

"A *Christmas* tree, Anne! I told you of the tree I saw in the family apartments at the embassy. How kind—how *good* of Mr. Davenant!"

Anne looked rather alarmed and very much at a loss as to what to say or do next. She was rather certain Arthur would not much relish returning home to find a tree in his drawing room. "Nerissa! You don't mean to put that— that tree in the house! Arthur won't stand for such nonsense!"

"Don't be such a faintheart!" Nerissa said bracingly. "Arthur won't mind once he sees how beautiful it is when it's decorated. Please, Anne, say we may keep it!" She didn't wait for an answer, but turned to Henry and said, "In the sitting room, if you please. And I think it should stand between the front windows. Bellamy, do move the settee so we may put the tree there!"

"I cannot like this!" said Anne worriedly.

"Please don't fret, Anne! Indeed, having a Christmas tree is an old German custom!"

"But *we're* not German!" insisted Anne, up in arms. "And when Arthur discovers a *tree* in his drawing room, he shall be quite furious! Of a certain, he will lecture us both about his position and how our conduct must be beyond reproach!"

"He won't be furious once he sees how it looks when it is decorated," said Nerissa with confidence. To the remainder of her sister's arguments she paid no heed, busy as she was guiding the steps of Henry and the footmen as they carried the tree up the stairs and into the drawing room.

As the men worked to prop the tree in place, Nerissa went to her writing desk and scribbled a hasty note to Mr. Davenant, begging him to wait upon her at his earliest convenience. She dispatched one of the footmen to deliver it, then she turned her attention toward soothing Anne's misgivings about having a tree in her house and devising a plan to make her Christmas tree just as lovely as the one she had seen at the embassy.

Chapter 10

Breck arrived at Bridgewater House later that afternoon, as a result Nerissa's message. His curiosity, rarely piqued, was running at a good-paced clip. He couldn't remember the last time anyone had summoned him so. Since Henry had not yet returned to report that he had delivered the tree as ordered, Breck could not guess the reason Nerissa would beg him to wait upon her on a matter, as she described most dramatically in her note, of the utmost urgency.

He entered the house to the sounds of merry laughter coming from the first floor drawing room. He thought for a moment that he had intruded upon a party. When Bellamy assured him that he was expected, he handed over his hat, gloves, and caped driving coat to a waiting footman.

He climbed the stairs in Bellamy's wake and paused upon the threshold for the barest of moments before Bellamy announced him.

All the occupants of the room were gathered around the Christmas tree, which had been erected between a pair of windows that looked out over the street. Arthur was standing upon a small, wobbling stool, the better to reach the top of the tree, where he was attempting to hang from its upper branches some small cloved apples. Anne stood below him, laughing and handing him apples and insisting, despite his best efforts, that he had missed a spot. Lord Crompton was defying the stiff confines of his shirt points to swivel his head first this way, then that, as he laced a string of cowberries through the lower branches. Nerissa and another young woman Breck didn't think he had never seen before were fashioning lengths of ribbon into festive bows.

Even Henry had been pressed into service, and was busily tying pine boughs together to be hung as valances over the windows on either side of the tree.

Breck stood for just a moment, taking in the cheery scene. He had thought, upon first entering the house, that he had been able to know the sound of Nerissa's laughter from all others' when he had heard it from the entry hall. He watched as she laughed again, a happy, musical laugh that complimented her shining brown eyes and glowing countenance.

The room was a hubbub of conversation and merriment when Breck entered. But when Bellamy announced him, everyone fell to startled silence.

Breck stepped into the room, and his gray eyes swept over it. Both Lord Crompton and Henry looked uncomfortable and rather embarrassed to be discovered in such a pastime. Lady Bridgewater and the unknown young lady were wearing rather stricken expressions of alarm. Lord Bridgewater swiveled around quickly and frowned.

Only Nerissa seemed wholly pleased to see him. She met Breck's gaze, and while her laughter fell away, her smile increased. She dropped the ribbons she had been working and went to him, saying, "Here you are at last! Thank you so much! Of course I would have known this was your doing even if Henry hadn't delivered it himself. Thank you! You see how beautiful it will be once we've finished decorating it!''

She held out her hand to him. He took it and looked down into her brown eyes, shining bright with happiness and gratitude.

"I thought you might be pleased, but I never thought you would make a party of adorning the thing," he said, quizzing her.

"How could I help but do so, when you see how beautiful it will be!'' Nerissa replied irrepressibly. She drew him farther into the room, saying, "Do come in and help us decorate the tree. You know everyone here, I think.''

"Do I?'' he asked in a lowered voice, his attention fixed upon the unknown young woman.

Nerissa followed his gaze and whispered, "That is Miss Farnham. You met her at Lady Willingham's dinner party! You must say something to her or she shall consider herself dreadfully snubbed!''

This he did, however briefly. Miss Farnham, deeply aware that she was in the presence of a leader of fashion she had been taught to revere since she had made her first curtsies, managed a nervous but proper reply.

Breck next bestowed the same degree of offhanded attention upon his cousin. He sketched the merest of nods and recommended that Lord Crompton mind where his decorating efforts had left a thin trail of berry juice along his sleeve.

"Egad! And this is a new coat too!'' said his lordship, examining the damage.

"What a shame!'' said Anne sorrowfully. "It's such a beautiful coat, Lord Crompton, and it looks so well on you. Come with me and we shall try to repair it.''

Arthur stepped down from his wobbling perch, a small frown between his brows. "Anne, there's no need to go off with Crompton. Let Bellamy take care of it.''

"We won't be long,'' she said sweetly. "Come, Lord

Crompton. Let us see if we cannot find some method that will take the stain out."

"I doubt there is much chance of that," said his lordship pessimistically, but he did follow Anne from the room.

Arthur glanced quickly at his other guests and gave a short, nervous laugh. "She *will* insist on mothering everyone!" he said. Then he came forward to shake hands with Breck. "I'm glad you're here, Davenant. You've arrived just in time to take over decorating the top branches of this tree. You see, I've managed to place the apples almost to the top."

Breck put his hands up to ward off any involvement in their decorating task, but found instead that a bowl of apples had been thrust into his hands. "I didn't come here to intrude on your party," he said, eyeing the bowl dubiously.

"But you must help us," said Nerissa, "for you are the only one who is tall enough to reach the top of the tree. You have only to place a few more!"

He couldn't very well refuse when she stood looking up at him with such an absurdly happy expression on her face. Nor could he ignore the rather cheeky look his tiger cast him from the other side of the room. He promised himself he would have his revenge on Henry later, and began to hang the last of the apples among the topmost tree branches.

He felt a trifle self-conscious—silly, to be precise—to be decorating a pine tree set in the middle of a fashionable London drawing room. Yet after a moment he forgot his own discomfort and focused his attention instead on watching Nerissa Raleigh.

He didn't think he had ever seen a happier or more optimistic young lady. She flitted from one person to another, giving instructions and commenting over the beauty of the tree and how festive the room was beginning to look. He watched her from the corner of his eye as she shepherded Miss Farnham and Arthur over to where Henry was still tying together pine boughs. She set them each to work attaching the ribbon bows to the pine boughs and joyfully instructed Arthur and Henry in the proper manner in which to hang them once they were complete.

She was, he realized with a good deal of amusement, a very managing sort of female, so when she turned her attention back toward Breck, he was quite interested to see if she had the nerve to instruct him with the same happy yet high-handed manner she had used upon everyone else.

She came to him with several lengths of ribbon draped over her shoulders and arms and said appreciatively, "You've done a very fine job of hanging the apples."

He looked down upon her and saw the glow of happiness in her brown eyes. "Have you any other tasks for me to perform?"

"Only if you think accepting my thanks to be a task! I'm grateful to you for all your kindness. You'll probably call me foolish, but I have been thinking about the Christmas tree we saw at the embassy. Truly, it was the most beautiful thing I have ever seen! It was a thoughtful gesture for you to give us this tree!"

"I thought you might like it," he said, having never quite been able to explain to his own satisfaction why he had felt so compelled to have sent it.

She took one of the ribbons from her shoulder and fashioned it into a bow. "Will you tie this to one of the branches above your head?"

He did, and felt her eyes upon him as he applied his fingers to the task. He asked in a casual tone, "Did you enjoy the rest of the ball after I left?"

She couldn't very well tell him that the remainder of the evening had paled considerably once he had taken his leave. She said instead, "We had a very enjoyable time. Arthur and Anne and I made many new friends, I think."

"I wasn't speaking of Arthur and Anne. I asked only after you. Did you dance after I left?"

He looked down at her and noticed a gentle flush had covered her cheeks.

She thrust another bow into his hands and said, "I danced the rest of the evening and sat out only once, when my feet hurt."

"Then you are quite a success," he remarked.

"I am indeed," she answered ingeniously. "One of my partners asked if he could kiss me."

Breck halted his task of tying a ribbon in place long enough to look down upon her with one brow cocked at an interesting angle. "Well? What did you say?"

"I said I didn't think I should like to share my first kiss with him. He took the news very well, I believe."

He had been prepared to be idly amused by her very innocent disclosures, but this startled him. "Do you mean to tell me you have never been kissed?" he asked, incredulous. "*Never*, Miss Raleigh?"

She shook her head. "No—and I cannot think why, because it seems to me that a girl my age should have been presented with at least *one* opportunity to be kissed!"

"Don't you think it's time you remedied the situation?" He looked down upon her upturned face, quite prepared to embark upon a round of tortuous teasing, but his attention was caught by the sweet curve of her lips and the tiny flecks of amber in the depths of her brown eyes. Suddenly he was struck by how lovely she was.

He was also a little stunned to realize that she was considering most seriously the words he had uttered in jest.

"Would *you* kiss me, please?" she asked.

He wasn't in the habit of being propositioned by virginal maidens, and she surprised a laugh out of him. "You *are* an innocent!"

"Why? Because I want to be kissed?"

"Because you think you have only to ask and it shall be so!"

She looked at him doubtfully. "Would it be so very bad to kiss me?"

"Oh, no! You'll not trap *me* with such a question!" he said, laughing slightly.

"I don't mean to trap you at all! But you were, after all, the one who suggested that I remedy my situation—"

"Remedy, yes! But don't expect me to play the doctor! Green girls, Miss Raleigh, are not at all in my line."

"I see," she said, quite unperturbed. "Are you very experienced? Have you kissed a good many women in your time?"

"I've kissed my share, I should venture to guess."

"Then would you please kiss me? I need someone to kiss me who is vastly experienced!"

He looked down at her with an incredulous expression. He didn't know whether to be outraged or amused, and said, "Despite what you may have heard about my reputation, Miss Raleigh, I don't go about kissing women on command!"

"Please don't be angry with me! I fear I'm saying this very badly, but you were the one who brought up the subject of kissing, you know!"

"Had I any notion at the time where this conversation was going to lead . . ." he began ominously.

"You're still worried that I have some sort of design on you, aren't you? You're still thinking that I have set my cap for you. I assure you, Mr. Davenant, nothing could be further from the truth. I want you to kiss me only for research purposes! I merely want to be able to see what it is like to be kissed. And if, as you say, you are an expert at kissing—"

"I never said anything of the kind!" he retorted, wondering when and how he had ever lost control of the conversation.

"But you did say you were experienced," she insisted, "and I must be kissed at least once in my life if I am to write convincingly of it in my book."

He took another bow of ribbons from her. "So we're

back to that, are we? I thought we already had this discussion, Miss Raleigh."

"I'm resigned to the fact that you won't help me by posing as a model hero. But I should think a simple kiss might be something you would be willing to help me with. After all, it will take only a moment."

He stared down at her, a hard look of consternation in his eye. She certainly appeared to be serious. "I'm afraid I cannot accommodate you, Miss Raleigh, enjoyable though the task might be."

"I didn't expect that I was going to enjoy it very much," she said candidly. "But I did expect that I should have to write down quite a few notes after it was all over."

He felt his temper rise slightly. He had long suspected that Miss Nerissa Raleigh was a young lady out of the common way. From the moment she had first padded after him on the street, he had been alternately amused and nettled by her behavior. But in this matter he was wholly thrown off his stride. He had a reputation with the ladies and prided himself on being a consummate lover. But he was a little stunned to realize that she held him in no more regard than she would a laboratory specimen.

It was something of a crushing blow to think that she wasn't interested in him at all but only in his capacity as a mannequin to be observed or to provide her with a new experience. He thought that she was very young and had many lessons to learn about life. She was a little too trusting, a little to *coming* for his tastes. And he had no doubt she would find herself in trouble one day because of it.

He was given an opportunity to see that prophecy borne out the very next afternoon. The morning fog had dissipated, and the day, while clear, was crisp and cool. He was driving up Piccadilly, when he spied Nerissa coming out of a shop. She was very correctly accompanied by a maid, who toted several packages as she followed in her mistress's wake. Nerissa's usually smooth, clear brow was furrowed in a frown, and her expression was far from happy as she walked down the street, casting worried glances about.

Had she been riding in a carriage, she might have felt a bit safer, but she had elected to leave her carriage behind and walk in the relative warmth of the bright December sunshine as she moved from store to store. She regretted having done so.

It had never occurred to her that walking Piccadilly with only a maid as a companion would prove to be less than safe, but after having been approached within the last twenty minutes by two separate gentlemen intent upon engaging her in conversation, she was forced to admit she had made a grave error in judgment.

She was again dressed in her cloak and hat of deep blue and she carried a small sable muff to protect her gloved hands from the chill. Her cheeks were flushed slightly from the cold and her full lips were tinged a very lovely cherry color. She presented, in fact, such a charming picture as she walked along the street that many of the vendors and passerby turned to watch her graceful progress. Their scrutiny, coupled with the unwanted advances of the two gentlemen, had left her feeling quite ill at ease.

Breck drew up before her and touched his gloved hand to the brim of his hat. "Miss Raleigh, a pleasure. As usual, you are attracting a bit of notice, I see."

To his surprise, she reached up and gave him her hand, saying, "Mr. Davenant! I am so very glad to see you! I have been shopping, you see, and I have left my carriage to walk and I *truly* wish I had not done so. It is only just around the next corner. Would you be kind enough to escort me to it?"

"Has something occurred to frighten you?" he asked, frowning.

"Yes! I mean, no! It is only that when I used to walk in our village at home, I was never stared at so!"

"I can't believe that—unless all the bucks in your village are either blind or in their dotage!"

"Then will you accompany me, please?" she asked very prettily.

"No, but I'll drive you to your door," he replied. "Henry, accompany Miss Raleigh's maid back to her carriage, will you? I'll meet up with you at Bridgewater House."

Henry obediently jumped down and assisted Nerissa up into the curricle. As soon as she was settled beside Breck, he draped a heavy rug across her legs and set his curricle in motion.

She sat quietly beside him for a few moments, watching him control his horses with an easy strength. "I'm so very glad you happened along. I feel much safer now that I'm with you!"

Breck withdrew his attention from his spirited pair just long enough to cast her a sidelong look. "Frankly, I'm not sure I like hearing a woman say that."

"But you should! If you hadn't happened by just now, there's no telling how many more dreadful advances I should have been forced to endure!"

"Advances? Do not tell me you have been accosted on the street?"

"Twice. And I believe the second man was a Cit," she said. "I don't think he was a gentleman at all."

"Neither was the first," Breck assured her.

"On the other hand, you are *always* a gentleman," Nerissa continued approvingly. "I am convinced you would never make a lady feel the least uncomfortable."

He glanced down at her. "Wouldn't I?"

"Oh, no! I have met you on several occasions now, and you have never made the least push to be excessively charming. You have never flirted or tried to make love to me. I don't think you could ever make a lady tremble merely by taking her by the hand!"

He was silent for a moment. "I see," he said at last. "Pardon me while I gather the shards of my male ego!"

"Have—have I said something wrong?" she asked, suffering the odd notion she had offended him somehow. "Do you *want* to make ladies tremble?"

As Breck knew himself to be something of a renowned success with the fairer sex, he was able to say most amiably, "Never, my innocent—although there are some ladies who profess to enjoy my company."

"I'm sure they do," she replied dulcetly. "Anne mentioned you were a prime catch. She said every eligible young lady had at one time or another set her cap for you."

"Yet you insist that the list of eligible ladies doesn't include you!"

"Oh, no! I have no designs on you, believe me! Much as I admire you for literary purposes, I would no more want to marry you than I would wish to marry either of those two horrid men who approached me on the street!"

He was rather at a loss to know how to reply to this stunning revelation. He should have been outraged that Miss Nerissa Raleigh should class his romantic skills on the same level as those of a Cit and a street-strolling Lothario. He found, instead, that he was more interested in knowing why she held the idea of marrying him—or any man—in such low esteem.

"If you dislike suffering such advances, you would do better not to go walking without a male attendant until the Season begins. By the way, how is it you came to be strolling the streets of London in the first place? Did you spot yet another example of the perfect gothic hero and decide to follow him?"

"I wish you wouldn't twit me about that," she said earnestly. "I know it was wrong of me to follow you as I did. But when I saw you driving your curricle, I recognized in you the very herolike qualities I had been looking for!"

Had any other person of his acquaintance made such a preposterous comment, Breck Davenant would have known him for the liar he was, but when he glanced down at Nerissa and met her absurdly innocent gaze, he realized that she was speaking nothing but the truth.

In her wide brown eyes he saw reflected honesty and warmth, and a hint of some emotion curiously akin to admiration. It startled him into saying quite firmly, "Miss Raleigh, I am no hero!"

"I think you are," she said confidently.

"Why? What is it that makes you so certain of my character?"

"I can't explain it, really. There is something in your disposition that makes you the perfect hero. You have such an easy air of authority and your manners are impeccable. I have been on hand to watch you orchestrate the behavior of those about you without them even realizing. Everything you do is of the very first order!"

"I think you've just described any number of very efficient butlers," said Breck with a half-smile.

"Your may laugh as you like," she said rather stiffly, "but I am well aware that a butler can never be confused with a true gothic hero!"

"The same can be said of me. I have more often been called a worthless fribble than a hero, Miss Raleigh!"

"I don't think that can be," said Nerissa. "Everyone I have met speaks quite deferentially of you. Even your aunt and your cousin follow your lead."

"Their opinion is of no importance to me!"

"That's your reckless streak talking," she said with a knowing look. "I believe all heroes hold little regard for the opinions of their relatives. On the other hand, I should not be at all surprised to discover that you are very protective of your family and the honor of your name."

"Young lady, you are crediting me with virtues I have never possessed!"

"Do you think so? I don't! Just now when you came upon me—did you think it was mere coincidence that brought us together today? You saved me just now from having to endure the hateful advances of strangers. It was very heroic of you, and I have a feeling you are more often heroic than you may know!"

He frowned slightly, feeling a bit discomfited by her words. "Just what *were* you doing walking along Piccadilly?"

"I was purchasing writing paper. We writers use quite a bit of it, you know."

"Working on your book, eh? Tell me, how many pages have you written? And when will this literary tome of yours be finished?"

"It is already finished, but the hero in the story must be altered a little. I am working most diligently to make the changes Mr. Heble, the publisher, has recommended. I mean to have it back to him by Christmas."

He frowned again as a memory from their very first conversation came back to him. "Why? Why is it so important that your book be purchased by Christmas?"

"Because if Mr. Heble buys my book, and if it is hugely successful, I shall be able to earn a very respectable income from it. With my own income, I shall be very independent and I shall not have to endure a Season and find a man to marry."

He gave a short laugh that held little humor. "Do you seriously expect me to believe you don't want to marry?"

"Of course! It is the truth, after all."

"That's nonsense! Every young woman wants a husband. Only look at your sisters!"

"Believe me, I have! They are all most unhappily wed. Why, even Anne cannot count herself happy, although I will grant you she is sometimes content, for Arthur is very kind to her. But she doesn't *love* him. Why, she hardly knows him!" said Nerissa in a voice of high tragedy.

Breck was silent for a moment, then he said in a thoughtful tone, "You know, I have half a notion you are serious."

"Very much so! I could never wed a man for his title or wealth, as my sisters did before me."

"Then you might have saved yourself the trouble of coming to London."

"I would have, most gladly! But my mother insisted I come. She thought I could use a little town polish and sent me to stay with Anne until the Season begins. Mama is very insistent that I take, you see. All the Raleigh sisters contracted brilliant proposals before the end of their first Season. My mother expects that I shall do the same."

"Tell her you don't want to do it," he recommended.

"That is much easier said than done. I'm afraid I am no match for my mama. She can be very compelling, you see. Since she is not at all in love with my papa after so many years of marriage, I don't think it ever occurs to her that her daughters might wish to be in love with their husbands."

"I suppose it would be Dutch comfort to tell you that your mother is not unusual. You'll find many women of society feel the very same way she does and are very willing to view marriage as a rather mercenary means to an end."

"But that doesn't make it right. I'm convinced *you* would never marry anyone merely for their title or fortune!"

"The circumstance shall never arise. I am rarely compelled to do anything I don't want to do."

"There! You have spoken as a true hero," said Nerissa appreciatively. "Only a man of herolike proportions could be so assured. I dare say you would never marry for the wrong reasons because you hold to your own very unique code of honor! It is not easy to go against convention or the wishes of another. You're very brave."

No one, in all Breck Davenant's one and thirty years, had ever spoken to him so. Honor, bravery—never to his knowledge had those two words ever been ascribed to him. He was oddly and somehow wholly flattered that this absurdly romantic young woman should think him capable of such idealism.

He looked down upon her briefly, an unreadable expression in his light gray eyes and the hint of a smile lifting the corners of his mouth. The smile grew, and he let out a laugh. "By God, I'll do it!"

She smiled back, hopeful, but hardly able to credit she had heard him correctly. "Do you mean you will help me after all? Tell me truthfully now! It would be cruel to tease me."

"I'm not teasing you—not this time, at any event," he said with another laugh. "While I have little doubt I shall very soon regret ever having embarked upon this folly, I am, as of this moment, at your disposal."

He allowed his gaze to settle briefly upon her and saw that she was looking up at him with an expression of absurd happiness.

"I am very much indebted to you!" she said warmly. "I promise not to be a nuisance in any way. I shall merely observe you and ask questions. I shan't trouble you more than is absolutely necessary."

"Then we have a bargain," said Breck in excellent humor. "What is your first question?"

"Well, let me see. I should need to know how you spend your time and if you gamble away exorbitant sums on a single turn of a card. And if you have any horrid secrets, such as a mad wife locked away in a garret room or a mistress with a mind to murder you—"

"Unlikely, I assure you!" he interrupted in an outraged tone. "A mere moment ago you were reading off a catechism of my sterling qualities. Now you think me capable of such beastly behavior?"

"But that is the sort of thing one might expect from a true gothic hero," said Nerissa reasonably. "Only consider *Glenarvon!*"

He frowned. "Is that the sort of poison you intend to write?"

"It's not poison," she returned rather defensively. "My story is an exposé of human frailties that encompasses emotions of epic proportion!"

In the face of this rather histrionic rejoinder, it was all Breck could do to keep from laughing. "You'll find that my emotions are rather limited and my frailties—you may depend upon it—are hidden very well away!"

She did her best to mask her disappointment. "You would make things much easier if you were something of a libertine with an impassioned but star-crossed love for a beautiful young woman." She had a sudden thought, and asked, "Who was the woman I saw you speaking with at Lord Kendrew's political reception?"

He searched his memory. "Mrs. Sodington. She is a longtime acquaintance."

"You were flirting with her," said Nerissa as she quite vividly recalled the evening, "and she appeared quite willing to accept your advances. Tell me, were you trying to seduce her?"

He was thrown quite off his stride. "Of all the impertinent—! Just what in blue blazes makes you think you may ask such a question?"

"Please don't be angry with me for asking. Truly, I think no less of you for it! You see, if you were a true gothic hero, you would seduce the poor woman, use her abominably, and discard her for a new, younger conquest!"

He was dutifully appalled by this innocent disclosure, and the thought occurred to him that he would very soon regret his decision to help Nerissa.

"Let us make sure we are in complete agreement as to my involvement in your scheme, Miss Raleigh," he said very sternly. "My understanding was that you wanted to use me as your *model*—not write *about* me. There's a difference, you know. I'm quite willing to let you see for yourself my makeup, but you must promise to preserve my anonymity when it comes time to write your story! And you're not to tell anyone that I had a hand in helping you. Do you understand?"

"I understand," she said obediently.

"Then, it's agreed?"

She looked up at him with what he was learning to recognize as a most bewitching smile.

"Agreed! May we start now?"

"Of course," he said, restored to good humor.

"What shall we do first?"

He wasn't at all sure how to answer her question, for he really had no idea on earth how a hero behaved. He had never before experienced the dubious pleasure of having someone idolize him, and he was rather at a loss to know how to proceed.

"I suppose I could show you how to drive to an inch," he offered gamely.

"Excellent! After all, your skill with a curricle and pair is what attracted my attention to you in the first place! What else?"

He cast his mind about quickly. "I have some skill with a pistol, and I could give you a very credible demonstration of swordplay if you'd like."

She clasped her hands together very tightly in an effort to contain her excitement. "Perfect! And will you wear a patch over one eye and walk with a limp as if you had been *severely* wounded in a duel?"

"Certainly not!" he retorted, a bit alarmed. "Of all the cork-brained ideas!"

"Are you an expert at fisticuffs?" she asked, unabashed. "Will you show me all you know about fighting? I promise you shan't regret it!"

"I regret it already!" he said with heartfelt sincerity, "and I am much alarmed that a delicately bred young woman such as you would wish to know such things!"

She touched his arm very lightly to draw his attention. "Perhaps it would help if you could forget I am a woman."

"Unlikely, I assure you!"

"But this is research! I promise you, my interest is purely scientific. Once I am through observing your behavior, we shall never have occasion to meet again."

"I rather doubt that prospect, Miss Raleigh!"

"You may call me Nerissa if you like," she said, looking

up at him with one of the most enchanting expressions he had ever seen.

He loosened his strong grip on the reins and allowed his high-couraged pair to pick up their pace. "I suppose," he said resignedly, "the sooner we embark upon this madness, the sooner it shall be over and done. First things first, Miss Raleigh. I believe I promised to show you how to drive to an inch."

Nerissa's brown eyes sparked with anticipation. "Excellent! I have longed to fly down the street in your curricle, just as I have seen you do! Is there anything special I must do?"

"Yes—hang on," he said as he negotiated the next corner with breathtaking precision.

It took every ounce of strength Nerissa possessed to keep from squealing. Their pace was recklessly fast as the curricle darted through the London traffic. Yet never for a moment did Nerissa doubt Breck's ability to navigate them safely around any crowd or obstacle.

His long, lean fingers held the reins with a sure, quiet strength, and his expression, visible from beneath the brim of his hat set at a jaunty angle across his forehead, was full of purpose.

Surely, she thought, there wasn't another more splendid example of masculinity in all of England than Mr. Breck Davenant. And now that he had agreed to help her, Nerissa vowed that she would make very sure to use him to the fullest extent.

Chapter 11

In the long gallery at Bridgewater House the very next afternoon, Breck Davenant brought Nerissa Raleigh's fencing lesson to an unexpected and abrupt halt.

"Enough!" he said impatiently. "There is no use pleading with me, for the answer is still no!"

He had stripped off his form-fitting coat, the better to teach her the proper manner in which to grip the foil. His hand had helped position her slim fingers over the hilt, and when her wrist had sagged from holding the unaccustomed weight, he had stepped up behind her to grip her wrist, adding his strength to hers. Thus he stood, with Nerissa's delicate frame backed against him, his long arm extended out with hers and her shining black curls nuzzling against his chin.

"Please, won't you reconsider? I don't see any harm in it, truly," Nerissa coaxed, turning just enough to look up at him with an impossibly naive light to her brown eyes.

Breck doubted very much that Miss Nerissa Raleigh ever failed to get her way whenever she directed just such a gaze toward another living creature. Heaven knew, *he* was having a deuce of a time resisting her.

He let loose his hold of her and took a few steps away, and said with as severe a tone as he could manage, "You are wasting your breath. No matter how beguilingly you may beg, I will not take you to a gaming den and I shall never smuggle you into a boxing saloon!"

"Then how am I to learn of such things?" she asked reasonably. "How am I to describe Count du Laney's foray into a gambling hell unless I have seen one firsthand?"

He frowned slightly. "Who the devil is Count du Laney?"

"He is the hero in my book. I told you that before," she said in a mildly accusing tone. "He is the very sort of character who would gamble away a fortune, then kidnap an heiress and force her to marry him just to replenish his coffers! So you see, I must know about gaming and such things."

"You would do better to write about him attending church services on Sunday," Breck recommended darkly. "You shall not learn of such things from me. I have been many things in my lifetime, but a corrupter of innocents, I am not!"

"I am not an innocent," Nerissa replied in a tone that did little to hide her keen disappointment.

Breck's anger abated slightly. She was as innocent as a lamb, but he didn't think she would at all relish being told so. He said instead, "Let us not argue! My mind will not be changed on this, Nerissa, so you may save your pleas. Now, shall we continue your instruction in the finer points of swordplay?"

She wanted to argue with him, or at the very least plead with him to take her to some dangerously masculine haunt. But the rather pointed look he cast her convinced her she would be better served to let the subject drop.

Nerissa picked up the foil and assumed the stance Breck had shown her earlier. "I have been told ladies are allowed to gamble in London," she said, unable to stop herself from arguing the point just a bit more. "Lady Willingham told me so."

"Lady Willingham is a married woman with a certain level of social cachet. Now, pay attention, brat. You are allowing your shoulder to drop."

He stepped behind her and, placing his strong hands on both her arms just above the elbows, he forced her to straighten her back and stand as he had shown her before. "Head, straight; shoulders, relaxed. Keep your arm up." When she didn't respond immediately, he placed his hand over hers on the hilt and drew the foil up to the height of her shoulder.

When he felt her curls tickle his chin, he realized he had once again rather unconsciously maneuvered her within the crescent of his arms. He looked down at her: at her midnight curls shining in the light of the late afternoon sun; at her small, fair hand, still enveloped within his.

Nerissa's delicate frame easily molded against him, and she had only to move her head ever so slightly to know the feeling of resting her cheek upon his shoulder. She could feel the warmth of Breck radiating through the fine linen of his shirt, and there was no mistaking the strength of his arms as they formed a half-circle about her. Truly, she thought, this was the most thrilling lesson she had ever had.

To her untrained senses, Breck smelled of masculinity; of musk-and-vanilla sweet waters and fine, aged tobacco. She felt the warmth of his breath stir her curls, and she wondered, for just a moment, what he would do if she moved against him and pressed her smooth forehead against the male roughness of his chin.

Nerissa tilted her head back slightly, exposing the tender white column of her neck. She looked up into his gray eyes. "Please don't think I am ungrateful for what you have shown me," she said in a voice that sounded breathless even to her own ears. "Truly, if I am overly eager to observe everything about you, it is only because I have never before met any gentleman as—as *admirable* as you!"

Breck Davenant was a man of experience; he was a veteran of a lengthy list of romantic conquests; but at that single moment he quite honestly could not remember ever wanting to kiss a woman as much as he wanted to kiss Nerissa.

Perhaps it was her ridiculous romantic notions, or her naive insistence that he was the stuff of heroes; but for one brief, overwhelming instant he wanted nothing more than to kiss her.

She moved slightly against him, and a most primitive response stirred within him. Only the knowledge that she was blissfully innocent of the profound effect she was having on him kept him from abandoning the fencing lesson for the more fulfilling prospect of teaching her what it was like to be properly kissed.

He forced himself to concentrate on her words. "You wouldn't say such things if you knew me well," he said, his voice low and resonant. "I am not at all admirable and I'm very rarely a gentleman!"

He had, in fact, come alarmingly close to showing her how ungentlemanly he could be. He let go of her and stepped away again, to put some distance between himself and the temptation of her lips.

Oddly, Nerissa felt a rather keen disappointment as she watched him move aimlessly away. She also felt no small amount of relief. Too late had she realized the nearness of his handsome face to hers as she stood within the circle of his arms. As he had held her, stock-still within his thrall, she had begun to feel breathless and a little lightheaded. Hardly the reactions of a woman who, for research purposes only, was observing the actions of a model hero.

She watched him a moment and noted a grimness to his expression that she tried to dispel with a light forced laugh. "You have told me so on many occasions! I don't suppose it would do any good for me to tell you once again that I believe quite the opposite? That you are quite the most *splendid* male specimen I have ever met?''

He frowned slightly and said in a low voice, ''What a curious young woman you are! I've just spent the major part of the afternoon describing to you my drinking and gaming haunts and still you think me admirable! You are a singular young woman, Miss Nerissa Raleigh.''

As there was no disapproval in his tone or censure to his expression, she cocked her head and smiled back at him. ''Singular *and* adept at swordplay. Thanks to your lesson, I have a very good idea of how to properly run a man through! Pray, what shall we do next?''

''I'm afraid your lessons have come to an end—for today, in any event.''

She had a difficult time hiding her disappointment. ''Why? Must you go?''

''Yes. I have a previous engagement, you see.'' He picked up his coat from a chair and began to shrug his broad shoulders into it.

''With whom?''

''No one you know.''

''Are you meeting Lady Sodington?'' asked Nerissa with an eagerness to pry into his romantic life that struck him as rather alarming.

''No, and I'll thank you to limit your questions to my sporting life!'' He saw her expression fall and immediately regretted the haste with which he had spoken. He said in a much milder tone, ''As it happens, I am to dine with a friend, then we are out for an evening of entertainment.''

''Where will you and your friend go for entertainment?'' She saw him hesitate, and said quickly, ''I am asking in a purely professional capacity, I assure you!''

''Very well,'' he said slowly and with an eye to her reaction. ''We will no doubt be at one of the gaming dens I described to you earlier, or perhaps at the Westminster Pit.''

Her interest quickened. "What happens at the Westminster Pit?"

"A fight," he said evasively.

"Excellent! Will you take me with you?"

"Certainly not! That is no place for a lady, and I regret having mentioned it in the first place! Really, Nerissa, you must cease pestering me to take you every place I mention."

"Please take me. It is of all things what I would like most to see."

"You said the very same thing when I told you about the Fives Court," he said very pointedly, "and Tothill Fields, *and* Fops' Alley."

"Yes, I know. But don't you see that I simply must know of these things? I have no brothers or uncles to observe, and you are such a *splendid* example of masculinity!"

"You could very easily be made to regret those words," he said grimly, "if only I were to give in to you. But the answer must be no! It is not a fit place for any young lady."

"Even if I were to go with *you?*"

"Do not suppose for a moment that any female could gain entrance! I dare say you wouldn't be admitted to such an establishment even if you were to present yourself dressed as a man! It's much too dangerous a place."

"Surely no harm could come to me if I were with you," she said with a confidence that made his expression soften.

Breck shook his head as he arranged the ruffled cuffs of his shirt that peeked from beneath the wrists of his coat sleeves. "You don't understand, my innocent, and you're much too young to have it explained to you. You have had your lesson in swordplay. Leave well enough alone for one day! I shall call on you tomorrow if you like."

He flicked a slight smile in her direction before he left the gallery. Nerissa thought there was just a hint of regret to the manner in which his eyes rested upon her, and his lips curved into that merest of smiles.

She wished for a reason to call him back, to compel him

to remain with her instead of leaving her for an evening of entertainment with a friend. She could think of no plausible reason to go after him, and had to content herself, instead, with going to the window and watching for him to quit the house. How much she wished she could climb up into his waiting curricle, behind that magnificent pair of horses, and tool the streets of London with a rakish flair. How much she wished she could accompany him that evening as he made his progress from one entertainment to another.

But he had very clearly forbidden her from accompanying him or learning any details of the evening he had planned for himself and his friend. Vividly did she recall his words: *You wouldn't be admitted to such an establishment even if you were to present yourself dressed as a man!*

Unfair! she thought. How on earth was she to learn of fights and amusements such as the Westminster Pit if she were never allowed to go there?

She was keenly frustrated. Somehow, she simply *had* to find a way to discover what Breck was doing that evening. Somehow, she had to learn firsthand how a very masculine and herolike gentleman passed an evening's entertainment. In one way or another, she needed to be admitted to those male milieux of which women had no knowledge. But his warning echoed in her ears: *You wouldn't be admitted to such an establishment even if you were to present yourself dressed as a man!*

From the window Nerissa watched Breck emerge from the house into the cold late afternoon and climb up into his waiting curricle. His hat was pulled low upon his head and his many-caped driving cloak hid his strong, muscled body from view. He was so shrouded against the cold that were it not for the unmistakable style with which he set his vehicle in motion, she might never have recognized him. Indeed, she could very well have donned his hat and coat and set off in his curricle herself. No one—not friend nor stranger—would have been the wiser.

You wouldn't be admitted to such an establishment even if you were to present yourself dressed as a man!

The notion came to Nerissa in an instant. She was a little bemused that she had not thought of it before. If she were to dress herself as a man, surely no one would recognize her! Surely, if her disguise were clever enough, she would be admitted to the Westminster Pit!

"Dare I?" she asked aloud, at once scared and dazzled by the notion. It took only a moment for her to decide. The temptation was too great and the lure too strong to be denied. She would see for herself what it was like to attend a sporting event as a man. She would discover for herself what men did to pass the time without the gentling influence of a woman.

And she would write about it. Yes! She would describe everything about the evening in the pages of her novel.

Nerissa quickly left the gallery and rang for Bellamy from the sitting room. "Where is Lord Bridgewater this afternoon, Bellamy?" she asked as soon as he answered her summons.

"I believe he is at his club, miss."

"And my sister, Lady Bridgewater? Has she returned from shopping yet?"

"No, miss. Since she asked that dinner be served at half past the hour tonight, I venture to think she shall be rather late from the shops."

"Excellent!" said Nerissa, thinking how easily the fates were aligning with her plan. "I shall be in my room, Bellamy, with the headache. And I shall not be disturbed for anyone. Is that understood?"

As it was far from Bellamy's place to question what he perceived to be a very feminine request, he said quite solemnly, "I understand, miss."

It was a relatively simple task for Nerissa to sneak into her brother-in-law's dressing room and secure for herself breeches and stockings; shirt and coat; cloak and cap.

She quickly discovered, however, that it was another task altogether putting on the pilfered items.

She had never before had occasion to don men's clothing. Having grown up in a household of women, she had, aside from her father, little experience with men's dress, and for some time she struggled with the unaccustomed articles. Once her disguise was complete, however, she discovered that she had done a most credible job of it. She could, indeed, pass most respectably as a young man. The breeches were only slightly too long, and the cloak, once fastened about her neck, effectively masked the fact that she had made a hopeless muddle of her neck cloth.

Nerissa remained in her room the rest of the afternoon, dressed in Arthur's clothes and waiting for the evening to advance enough that she might venture out under cover of darkness. Neither Arthur nor Anne knocked upon her bedroom door, and she offered up a silent word of thanks that Bellamy should have passed along her message so convincingly.

When the small mantel clock in her room struck nine, she felt it safe to leave the house. From habit, she knew that Anne and Arthur would be in the small sitting room after dinner, sharing a companionable silence, with Arthur's nose in a book and Anne stitching at her frame.

The rest of the house was quiet. Nerissa had little trouble sneaking out a door that gave off the dining room onto a small terrace. She circled the house and walked a little self-consciously down the street, fearful that she be recognized or that someone might know her for the fraud she was. When she had walked several blocks and realized she had attracted not the least attention, she felt more assured and confident. She had her pin money with her and she hailed a hansom cab as she had seen gentlemen do before.

With a conscious effort to make her voice as deep as possible, Nerissa instructed the jarvey to take her to the Westminster Pit, and hoped with all her being that he would know where the horrid place was.

He didn't question her over it, but he did look down upon her from his high perch as if she were a bug. "And I suppose, Mr. Fancy Lad, you'll have the lolly to pay me once I take you there?" he said pessimistically.

"Of course!" she answered quite promptly. "Shall—shall I pay you now?"

He gave her another long look, and this time it was accompanied by a frown. " 'Ere now, why'd you want to go there? You're mighty fresh to be asking to go to such a place as the Pit. If it's a bit of the home brew you be looking for, let me take you someplace else as would be more fitting. A nice mill, perhaps."

Nerissa made her voice as deep as possible. "I'm quite old enough, thank you. Now, will you take me there or not?"

He silently debated the question for several moments. "Get in, then," said the jarvey at last. And no sooner did Nerissa climb up on the small bench and draw the door across her lap than he gave his horse the office and they were off.

Chapter 12

What a delicious thing it is to be male, thought Nerissa as she stepped down from the hansom cab in front of a rather unprepossessing building. Surely, she reasoned, men had all the fun in, life for a man worried not for going out without a companion. A man could attend rather iniquitous entertainments, hail hansom cabs, and dress in comfort without skirts, garters, or petticoats.

She stood for a moment at the curb, savoring the sensation of freedom, and wondering—just briefly, mind—whether she might not have the courage to make a habit of dressing in Arthur's clothes and setting out for a bit of adventure on a somewhat regular basis.

She took a swift, appraising look about, saw several gentlemen enter the building, and knew the jarvey had brought her to the right place.

As she had seen men do before, Nerissa tossed her fare up to her driver, and saw that he was once again eyeing her shrewdly.

His steady scrutiny made her feel rather uncomfortable,

and she said dismissively, "Thank you. You may be on your way now."

"Not at all. I've a mind to wait awhile, I think," said the jarvey.

"In this cold?" she asked, watching the small cloud of frost that formed in the air with every breath. "There's no need, I assure you. I dare say I shall be here for some time."

"Mayhap you will—mayhap you won't. Still, I've a mind to wait a shake or two," he insisted.

In the face of such stubbornness, there was no use arguing with the man. Nerissa squared her slim shoulders and, invoking what she hoped to be a very masculine swagger, entered the building.

Her courage faltered as soon as she crossed the threshold and heard the solid oak door close behind her. She had half expected a setting much like a public house, with tables and chairs and a kindly landlord who would show her to a table, where she might refresh herself with food or drink. But the room in which she found herself could not have been further from the place of her imagination.

The Westminster Pit proved to be a large, dimly lit and smoke-filled room crowded with gentlemen from a variety of stations in life. There were a few tables circling the perimeter of the room, all occupied by men imbibing in spirits and ales and conversing in loud and rather coarse terms. But the place was dominated by a pit located in the center of the room and ringed all around by a low wooden wall.

Nerissa stood a moment, just inside the door, taking in her surroundings and feeling, for the briefest of moments, that she had made a grave error in judgment to have come to such a place.

As she stood wrestling her courage, a deep masculine roar rose up and the crowd of men pressed forward toward the railing of the walled pit, their glasses raised and their voices cheering. Nerissa pressed forward with them, and shouldered her way through the crush so she might be able to see for herself what everyone was staring at.

She gained the wall of the pit and looked down to see two dogs in the center of the ring. Lean and muscled animals, they circled each other with their ears back, teeth bared, and bristles up.

At first Nerissa thought some accident or error had brought the two animals together. Surely at any moment one of the gentlemen in the crowd or the owner of the establishment would reach down and pull the hapless dogs from the pit. But one glance about at the men assembled told her they intended to do no such thing. Instead, they pressed forward eagerly, their glasses raised, their voices chorusing.

Nerissa felt a trill of alarm as she wondered who would rescue the dogs from what appeared to be a quickly brewing fight. No sooner did that thought form than she saw one of the dogs pause in its tracks. The animal let loose a bloodcurdling growl and launched itself into battle.

The sickening noise of dogs fighting warred with the cheers of the men surrounding the pit. It was a frightening spectacle, and for a moment Nerissa could hardly believe she was witness to such a scene. Horrified, she glanced quickly around to see if anyone else was as repulsed as she. In the dim light of the room, she saw only the avid expressions of a crowd of men who were vastly entertained—and among them she saw Breck Davenant.

He was directly across from her on the other side of the pit, with a pint of bitters in one hand and a cigarillo in the other. A gentleman standing next to him said something and laughed, but Breck's attention remained focused upon the action in the center of the room. Unlike the other men in attendance and his friend beside him, Breck didn't cheer or call out. He stood watching the dogs fight with the same languid pose with which he might have watched a chess match or a game of patience.

Nerissa could not feign the same indifference. Never

had she imagined that a hero's amusement could be so violent. A wave of revulsion shook her. She tried to look away, but she was hard pressed to decide whether she was more disgusted by the carnage in the pit or by the men who found entertainment in such a savage display. She was beginning to feel quite physically ill. The chorus of men's shouts rang in her ears and her head began to swim slightly.

She looked away, unable to stand watching the dogs another moment. As she looked up, she saw Breck again, and this time he was staring back at her as if he could not quite believe his eyes.

Had she not been so shocked by the grisly spectacle in the pit, Nerissa might have bolted for the door, or at the very least have pulled her cap lower over her eyes to conceal herself a bit more. But her legs had turned to jelly with the first wave of revulsion that had hit her, and the sickening dizziness had usurped her power to reason. She had no choice but to remain where she was, her knees trembling threateningly, and her eyes, wide with shock, staring back at Breck.

He left his friend without a word and made his way around the arena, shouldering through the throng of men with a grim purpose. Not once did he take his eyes from Nerissa. When at last he reached her side, he saw that her face had gone very pale and her full lips were trembling threateningly.

At that moment he could have very easily throttled her. He controlled the impulse and pressed his lips into a tightly gripped line. Without a word he clasped Nerissa's elbow and began to propel her through the crush of men toward the door.

Neither of them spoke. Nerissa was too upset and dangerously near to fainting, and Breck was too angry to trust himself to utter a single sound without betraying the depth of his feeling.

The hansom cab was waiting just as the driver had promised, and Breck dragged her toward it. He threw back the cab door with a violent force, and before Nerissa could move, he scooped her up in his arms and tossed her up onto the bench.

In the close confines of the cab, on a seat barely wide enough for the two of them, Breck wedged his considerable size in next to Nerissa and closed the door with a decided slam. Only when the vehicle was at last in motion did he trust himself to speak.

"How *dare* you come here?" he demanded in a thunderous voice. "I expressly forbade you to be here tonight!"

Nerissa could hardly speak, so great was her mortification. She managed to say in a voice that was little more than a strangled whisper, "I am sorry! I am *so* sorry!"

"As if that would cure it all! Have you any idea of the danger you were just in? Have you any notion of what might have happened had you been unmasked as a woman in that place?"

She choked on a sob and shook her head. "I had no idea! I had no notion men behaved so!"

"That's no excuse!" said Breck savagely. "Haven't I spent the better part of the last two days describing to you what kind of beasts men are? What in blue blazes made you think you could do such a thing?"

"I wanted only to see for myself—to have an adventure—oh! It was all so horrid!"

"Not as horrid as it might have been had you been discovered!" he said grimly.

"I had no notion, no idea at all! It was the most sickening spectacle! I felt quite ill, and if I had fainted—as I was half afraid I might—I would have been found out! Breck, I am so sorry! How could I have been so foolish?"

Breck's impatient mouth was set in a rigid line of anger that thankfully prevented him from answering her question.

But it did not prevent him from glaring down upon her. He had draped one arm along the back of the seat so he could turn slightly to face her. Nerissa was pressed against his side and was almost enveloped by the half-circle of his arm. She could feel the length of his body along her own, and his hard, muscled thigh was pressed against her hip. So near was he that with every word he spoke his breath touched her hair.

In the midst of his ravings, amid all the shock and panic of her own emotions, Nerissa began to feel a bare glimmer of peace. It didn't take long for her to realize that despite the danger of what had just occurred, she now felt quite protected and secure within the strong circle of Breck's arms.

A rather pleasant flicker of warmth sprang to life within her as she looked up into his pale gray eyes, half hidden by the shadows of the cab.

"You saved me," she said in a voice barely above a whisper. "Just now you rescued me from a very vile and dangerous fix."

Breck opened his mouth to respond, but found that he was quite thrown by the unexpected note of admiration in her voice. "Don't start that nonsense again," he said in warning.

"But it's true. You *did* save me," she insisted.

His anger rose again. "You little hoyden, have you listened to a single word I've said?" he demanded furiously. "If I was compelled to save you, it was only because I put you in such a dangerous predicament to begin with!"

"You're right," she said wretchedly. "It was wrong of me to follow you tonight. Will—will you ever forgive me?"

He heard the slight quaver in her voice and knew that she was very close to tears but fighting them bravely. He tucked a finger under her chin and forced her head back so he might look at her more clearly in the dim light of the hansom cab. Her brown eyes were moist and her chin quivered slightly. She blinked several times to fight back the betraying emotion.

"There is nothing to forgive," he said in a much gentler

tone as he pulled her cloak closer about her. "Perhaps I should not have railed at you just now. But when I think how close you came to ruin tonight, I could very well strangle you. Why, if something had happened to you, I—" He stopped short, unsure that he wanted to travel that path.

In fact, he wasn't at all sure of anything since having made the acquaintance of this tiresome girl. He had every right to be angry with her for having been foolish enough to have followed him when he had expressly forbid her to do so. He also knew an unaccustomed sense of guilt, as if he were somehow responsible for what had occurred.

He couldn't recall a time he had ever before accepted responsibility for anyone or anything. He had always operated by his own set of rules with regard for no one's comfort but his own. Wide-eyed Nerissa Raleigh, with her blind admiration and absurdly romantic notions, had changed all that without his even being aware.

There were few people for whom he had ever put himself out, even fewer for whom he might have been said to have rescued. He had once or twice come to the financial aid of a friend, but there was nothing to admire in that. He had been known in the past to have been instrumental in setting a certain opera dancer's feet upon the path to success with his patronage and generosity, but that sort of conduct was far from virtuous. The only person on whose behalf he could recall ever exerting himself was Nerissa, and he was damned if he could discern why.

She interested him, of that there was no doubt. He had been toad-eaten during his life by any number of social climbers who mistook him for a man who could be flattered into friendship. Nerissa flattered him, not with gushing words, but with a blind faith in his abilities. It had never occurred to her that he might be less than the man of her imagination. She seemed to take for granted that his every action was nothing less than heroic. For some odd and deeply confusing reason, he was loath to disappoint her.

The more he saw of her, the more proprietary he felt and the more desire to shield her from every danger. Even now, as she sat nestled within the circle of his arms, he felt very much like her champion. Good Lord, he thought, was it really possible that her absurd notions of heroes and romance had rubbed off on him? Could it be that he had ceased to be a jaded, world-weary man and turned instead into the hero she imagined him to be?

The lack of artifice with which she now looked up at him convinced him that she believed just so. There was a frankness in her expression, an innocent trust that made him at once wary and proud. He didn't think he wanted to be regarded as a true hero. Yet, if he were honest, he would have to admit he rather enjoyed being the object of her loyal, unwavering admiration.

It wasn't like Breck Davenant not to know his own mind, but Nerissa Raleigh had introduced an element of uncertainty to his life. At that very moment he wasn't sure which would give him more immediate satisfaction: taking her in his arms and kissing her soundly or heartily shaking some sense into that ridiculously romantic head of hers.

Thankfully, he was saved the trouble of making that decision as their vehicle pulled up in front of Bridgewater House.

"Can you manage to get back inside without being discovered?" Breck asked in a quiet voice.

Nerissa nodded. "I shall go in the same way I came out. Breck, I—" She stopped, debating for a moment the prudence of going on, then squared her shoulders purposefully. "Breck, I am truly sorry I disobeyed you and—and I thank you most *humbly* for saving me."

Even in the dark of the hansom cab, Breck thought there was no denying the sincerity of her expression. He trailed a finger down the softness of her cheek. "All is forgiven, my innocent."

"Then you aren't angry with me?" she asked, hopeful.

He had his answer then: he *did* want to kiss her, and he

controlled the impulse with an effort. It was almost a full minute before he could say in a voice of tolerable composure, "I'm not angry. Now, go into the house before we begin to attract attention here at the curb."

She obeyed him, but with the utmost reluctance. It was a difficult thing to leave the warm strength of his arms. As soon as Nerissa stepped down from the cab, she felt a little lost, a little abandoned.

He made no attempt to go with her, but he did wait in the cab until she had disappeared around the side of the house. As she disappeared from his view, Breck decided it would probably be a very good thing if he made a point to avoid Nerissa's presence in the future.

Chapter 13

Anne dropped her needlework to clasp her hands together in a very tight grip. She looked across the drawing room to where Nerissa sat at her writing table, her manuscript spread before her, and asked in a breathless voice, "Then what happened? Tell me quickly or I shall faint dead away!"

"Nothing else happened, I'm afraid," said Nerissa with a slight shrug to her slim shoulders. "Breck Davenant left me at the curb. I came into the house and went straight up to my bed."

"Do you mean to tell me he didn't kiss you?"

"No, he didn't. And, Anne, that was *two* nights ago! I haven't seen or heard from Breck since."

"Are you quite sure he was tempted to kiss you? Perhaps it was too dark in the cab, Rissa dear, to tell properly. Perhaps you mistook shadows for passion."

"I don't think so," said Nerissa, giving the matter no small amount of thought. "I think I am old enough to recognize when a man wants to kiss me. A woman knows these things."

"Then I wonder why he didn't, for yours is certainly a very romantic story. How daring you were! And how dashing he was to have rescued you so. But it was very naughty of you to have gone to such a place. Rissa dear, whatever possessed you to do it?"

"I don't know," she replied with a heartfelt sigh. "I wish I had not done so, for the dogfight was the most horrid spectacle! But, oh, Anne, Breck was so wonderful once we left—after he was done cutting up at me, that is. During the entire ride home he had his arm about me, and I felt so safe and warm with him. He was gentle and tender and—and—"

"Heroic?" offered Anne.

"Yes! No man could have been more so!"

"What a wonderful story! So often I have wished Arthur would behave in the same romantic and dashing manner. You're very fortunate to have captured the attention of such an ideal man, Rissa dear."

Nerissa looked up quickly. "I've not captured his attention. No such thing, I assure you!"

"Then why does Breck Davenant spend so much time with you?" asked Anne reasonably.

"He is helping me with my book, nothing more. Anne, you know all this!"

"Yes, but I also know about Breck Davenant—or, at least, I believe I know him from all the rumors I have heard concerning his behavior. It is generally reported from all quarters that he is a terribly selfish and often disobliging man. I must wonder, then, why he has taken such an interest in you. I must also wonder what he expects in return for his efforts."

"You're much too suspicious," said Nerissa, scoffing, "and you know as well as I do that Breck is nothing like the man you just described."

"Nerissa dear, has he ever said exactly what his intentions are toward you?" Anne asked with a pointed look.

Nerissa thought she had a very good notion what Breck's

intentions were, but she didn't think she had the courage
to voice that notion aloud. His intentions, she was sure,
were to abandon their friendship as soon as she relin-
quished him from his promise to help her. That prospect
held the power to send her spirits plummeting.

Over the past two weeks of her acquaintance with Breck,
he had formed the uncomfortable habit of intruding upon
her thoughts. This she had been able to discount by telling
herself these thoughts came as a result of her admiration
for him. She had, after all, long insisted that he was the
embodiment of the perfect male hero. But last night had
changed all that.

Last night, as she had left the safety and warmth of his
arms to sneak back into the house and put herself to bed,
Nerissa had realized that her feelings for Breck went far
beyond those of a writer for her subject. She had been
provided plenty of opportunity to dwell upon that realization. Sleep had eluded her until well into the morning
hours, and she had lay awake, vividly recounting over and
over again their carriage ride and glorying in the memory
of what it had felt like to have his arms around her.

It was a difficult thing for Nerissa to admit she was very
close to falling in love with Breck Davenant. It was impossible to admit it to Anne. Like her sister, Nerissa had heard
enough of the rumors concerning Breck's rather rakish
reputation to know that she was dangerously close to being
added to his list of conquests. He, however, did not at all
appear to be a man who cared for Nerissa any more than
for any other lady of his acquaintance.

Breck had never hinted that his feelings for her ran
any deeper than enjoyable companionship. Certainly, she
amused him, and she had sometimes thought that she had
caught for only a quick moment a look of genuine affection
in his usually cold gray eyes. A quick mental inventory of all
the times they had spent together provided little comfort.
Nerissa knew that for every instance in which Breck
behaved as if he did indeed care for her, there were just

as many occasions when he had spoken to her with indifference. Just what, exactly, he *did* think of her, she had never been given a hint. She rather thought that her feminine intuition would have detected any loverlike emotions on his part, if they did, indeed, exist.

It was beyond Nerissa's ability to confess these thoughts to her sister, for that would have meant admitting that while she was rather hopelessly drawn to Breck, he did not at all return her regard. That was something her pride would not allow her to do.

She squared her slim shoulders and gave a carefree trill of laughter. "Breck's intentions? He has none, I assure you! As soon as my book is complete—which, I dare say, should happen this very day!—Mr. Breck Davenant shall go on about his business, much as he did before we ever made his acquaintance."

Anne looked at her shrewdly. "What about you?"

"I shall be a famous authoress, just as I have always planned. Christmas is only days away. I promise you, Anne, by the time I awake Christmas morning, I shall have a commitment from Mr. Heble to purchase my book and I shall have enough money to support myself."

"Is that still your plan? To live your days alone in a garret with only your stories for companionship?"

"Of course! Truly, Anne, there is no need for you to sound so melancholy. Writing my stories is the only thing I have ever wanted to do in life, and it is certainly the only talent I have that may earn me a competent living. I cannot sing, my watercolors are abysmal, and my needlework is atrocious. Tell me, Anne, if I may not make my living as a writer, what else is there for me?"

"You could be presented, just as Mama plans you to be. We could start preparations for your first Season immediate on the new year, just as our elder sisters did."

Nerissa shook her head. In her heart she knew that a presentation could lead to only one thing: marriage. "Anne, we've discussed this before. You know very well I could never bring myself to contemplate the notion of marrying a man I didn't love."

"But once you have been presented and you are out, you might meet a man you could love," said Anne reasonably. "It wouldn't be difficult to do."

Nerissa rather thought it would be impossible. Having made the acquaintance of Breck Davenent, she didn't think she could ever find the least interest in another man, for no other man, she was sure, could ever measure up to Breck's shining example. But once again she was unable to summon the courage to make such an admission, and said, instead, quite candidly, "If it were not so difficult, why didn't *you* marry a man you loved?"

Anne stiffened slightly and said in a tight little voice, "Love is not something one can call up upon command, Nerissa. Sometimes love arrives rather unexpectedly."

"So I have heard, and I think what you just said is very true. That's why the plot of my book centers around a heroine who escapes a marriage with a man she doesn't love by running off with the hero, Count du Laney."

"I dare say your book will be quite scandalous once it's published," said Anne. "Thank goodness things like that could never happen in real life!"

"Don't they? I think they can and do! All it takes is for a spirited girl to decide she will not be trapped in a loveless marriage. I cannot speak from experience, but I rather think it's not that far to Gretna Green, if you are making the journey with someone who truly loves you."

Anne was very quiet for a moment, her needlework stilled in her lap. "Nerissa, do you truly believe the things you say?" she asked, her gaze quite intent upon her sister's face. "Do you believe, in fact, that a woman should risk all for the man she loves?"

"Of course! I may not be an expert on affairs of the heart, but every one of the novels you or I have ever read has been quite clear that true love is not something to be denied."

"And do you think," asked Anne slowly, "that a woman should *tell* a man she loves him if, indeed, those are her true feelings?"

"I'm not sure," said Nerissa with a slight, thoughtful frown. "In every novel I have ever read, the heroine doesn't declare her love until the very end of the story. But throughout the book she does *show* her love, and she's rather passionate about doing so too."

Anne picked up her needlework and began to set fine stitches with a slow but steady hand. She didn't speak for a long while, then she said in a low, fervent voice, "It's not always easy to know what is the right thing to do when it comes to love. In your case, Rissa dear, it's not too late for you to avoid making a mistake. I hope you'll be very careful of the decisions you make today, for they will have a powerful impact upon you tomorrow."

"I know very well the decision I shall make! With you and my other sisters as examples, I would wager I have very little chance of ever being truly happy in marriage. On the other hand, I would also be willing to wager I shall be exceedingly happy in my garret, writing adventurous stories with beautiful ladies and dashing heroes."

She was obliged to steadfastly repeat those brave words more than once in an effort to hide her disappointment. Breck did not call upon her at all that day, nor did he make an appearance that evening at a small musical recital that Nerissa attended with her sister. It wasn't until the next evening that she again met Breck, and even then she had cause to doubt whether he was at all glad to see her.

Arthur had secured a box at the Royal Opera House. They had arrived early enough to see and greet acquaintances and well-wishers before the curtain rose. It was Nerissa's first trip to the theater, and as she took her seat in the front row of the box, she gazed eagerly about, noting the dazzling finery of the audience and the theater itself. She was avidly studying all about her, when the door to the box directly across from theirs opened. Lord and Lady

Kendrew were ushered in, followed by Lord Crompton, and trailing behind at a languid and disinterested pace was Breck Davenant.

The performance began almost immediately after they were seated. What music was played, what opera was performed, Nerissa had little idea. She knew only that she was having a difficult time keeping her eyes focused upon the stage, for her attention kept wandering back across the theater toward Breck. She hadn't seen him since he had driven away in the hansom cab and she was rather nervous at the prospect of speaking with him again. They had parted brass rags, she knew. There had been no anger in his voice when he had bid her good night and handed her down at the curb, but neither had there been any gentleness or indication on his part that he had been as affected by her nearness as she had been by his.

She was rather well convinced that Breck was making a deliberate effort to stay away from her, and that could mean only that he had not yet forgiven her for her conduct. Once or twice she stole a look at him, and thought she saw his eyes upon her, but she could discern neither approval nor censure in his expression. She yearned to speak to him, to explain, if she could, the foolish reasons that had led her to breach the masculine walls of the Westminster Pit. But she could hardly be the one to approach him first, and she found herself wishing, with all her optimistic might, that he would make his way to the Bridgewater box at the first interval.

She was to have her wish. Breck and his cousin presented themselves as soon as the last note of music ended. Breck bowed politely and greeted them all with a look of cool civility.

Arthur stood and nodded a greeting. "Evening, Davenant. I didn't know you were an opera man."

"I'm not, actually. But there's curst little amusement in town at this time of year." He cast his polite but bored eyes upon Nerissa. "Miss Raleigh, do you enjoy the opera?"

It was an inane question, one that was hardly worthy of a man who in the past had made delightful conversation. In that brief question, Nerissa knew herself to be unforgiven.

She raised her chin a notch in a vain attempt to show herself and everyone around her that she wasn't at all hurt by his coldness. "I'm enjoying it very well. This is my first trip to the theater, you see. Arthur arranged it for us." She saw that Breck was looking down upon her with an expression of bland inquiry, and blurted out, "Arthur is quite wonderful! He—he is very knowledgeable too, and has explained the entire opera to me, since I don't speak Italian."

"And I've had a deuce of a time translating, I can tell you," said Arthur, laughing. "I read Italian in school, but I've forgotten most of it, to tell the truth. Anne is the linguist in the family," he added proudly, turning toward his wife.

But Anne had not heard a single word he had said, for no sooner had Arthur vacated his seat to speak with Breck than Lord Crompton had claimed the very same chair and, with it, Anne's attention. They were engaged in a conversation of low and furtive voices that could not be heard over the general noise of the room.

A dull flush of color mantled Arthur's cheeks as he turned back toward Breck and said with marked strain, "Anne is quite an accomplished young woman, you know."

At first Breck didn't reply. He saw no need to embroil himself in the little tragedy being played out before him. Arthur Bridgewater was a sensible young man not given to flights of fancy or rash behavior. If his wife was engaged in a flirtation, Breck believed, Arthur's common sense and level head would cause him to behave sensibly until the beastly business had played itself out.

But when he chanced to look down into Nerissa's brown eyes, he surprised a look of suffering there. If Nerissa were aware of her sister's conduct and troubled by it, Breck would have to intervene.

Why he should feel compelled to do so he had no idea. He didn't propose to tease himself over it. He knew only that he didn't like to see her unhappy, especially when it was quite unnecessary for her to be so.

Breck was an experienced campaigner when it came to pursuits and conquests in the field of love. He may have been observing Crompton's behavior with Anne Bridgewater through a bored but polite demeanor, but that didn't mean he had overlooked what to him was painfully obvious: Anne Bridgewater was not at all infatuated with his cousin. He could not be quite as sure of Lord Crompton's frame of mind, but he was fairly certain that Anne wasn't at all tempted to embark upon a dalliance in that quarter.

He was frankly relieved. Had there been more to the relationship, he would have felt compelled, for Nerissa's sake, to thrust a spoke in Crompton's wheel. As a rule, he didn't concern himself with such matters. But then, quite a few of his old rules had gone by the wayside since having made the acquaintance of Miss Nerissa Raleigh.

He looked at Arthur and said pointedly, "Lady Bridgewater is a lovely and accomplished woman, as you say. I believe she is as much admired for her good sense as she is for her beauty."

Apparently, Arthur saw nothing sensible about his wife's conversation with Crompton. He glanced quickly over at Anne, then mumbled a rather stiff apology and left the box without another word. To Breck's experienced eye he may not have been in high dudgeon, but he certainly had the appearance of an angry young husband as he bowed his way from the box.

Breck looked down at Nerissa's face and saw she still had that pensive look about her. Given a choice, he would have much preferred to see her looking up at him with that preposterous look of adoration in her lovely brown eyes. He asked softly, "Nerissa, is something wrong? Will you tell me what has upset you?"

More than anything, she wanted to. And with her sister

engaged in conversation and Arthur absent, she thought it safe to ask very quietly, "You're not still angry with me, are you?"

"Angry? Not at all. Why do you ask?"

"Because of what I did the other night. I know you were furious with me—and rightfully so! But you didn't come to visit yesterday or today, and just now, when you greeted us, I didn't think you were at all pleased to see me."

"You mistake," he said in a low voice that held a hint of a caress. "I am always pleased to see you."

Those simple words were enough to set Nerissa's heart singing. She smiled up at him with a look of unmistakable happiness. Breck, having long since resigned himself to being forever amused by her absurd optimism, found himself smiling back.

He had meant to keep her at arm's length, believing, after her reckless escapade at the Westminster Pit, that he had made a gross mistake in agreeing to her preposterous scheme to teach her about masculine pursuits. He had come to realize that he was, at best, a poor influence on such an impressionable girl. Without meaning to, he had provided her with some rather alarming notions, and he thought it might be a good idea to curtail his influence a bit.

But there was another reason he wanted to distance himself from Nerissa. From the moment he had handed her up into that hansom cab, Breck had felt oddly guilty and wholly responsible for having placed her in such a dangerous situation. Not quite immediately, but soon enough, he had begun to feel rather protective of her and more than a little proprietary. Try as he might, he could discover no reason for these unaccustomed feelings. Then it occurred to him that it just might be that Nerissa's absurd notions of heroes and romance were beginning to rub off on him; that he had begun to believe himself to be the hero of her imagination.

Could it be? It was a stunning thought for a man who

had always known an odd amount of pride in the fact that his reputation was one of a jaded and rather cold-hearted cur. But there was no mistaking the sudden warmth that swelled about his heart when Nerissa looked up at him with undisguised relief and said, "I am so glad to hear you say so! I was half afraid you were too vexed with me to carry on. You see, I think I have quite finished work on my book, and it would be such a disappointment if you were to cry off now, when I'm relying upon you to provide just one or two more details to make my story authentic."

For a moment he didn't reply. It was beyond his ability to admit he was a little hurt that her only interest in him was as an object of research. But as it was apparent that the performance was about to resume, Breck was not at all in a position to quiz Nerissa over her comments.

He briefly clasped her small, gloved hand and looked down upon her with his gray eyes once again hooded with disinterest. "Then I shall not fail you. I'll call on you tomorrow and take you driving, if the weather is fine enough."

"And if it isn't?" she asked with a look of quickened interest.

"Then you may be sure I shall find some method of instructing you in heroic behavior that doesn't present any sort of threat to you."

Arthur returned then, looking much more composed than when he had left them a few moments before. If his manner was a trifle stiff as he bowed to Breck and Lord Crompton from the box, it could not be said that it was less than proper. That he was jealous of Crompton's attentions toward Anne, Breck held little doubt, but Arthur was sensible enough to have put some distance between himself and the cause of his jealousy, and to cool his temper down and allow his good sense to prevail.

There was certainly a lesson to be learned there. Breck wondered whether it might not be a good idea to put some distance between himself and Nerissa. He didn't quite trust the unaccustomed feelings gathering in his heart and he wasn't quite sure what to make of them. He did know, though, that he was moving dangerously close to making a cake of himself over her. Perhaps it would be wise to take a page from Arthur's book; perhaps he would do better to put a bit of distance between himself and Nerissa. Yes, a little time apart might be the very thing he needed to cool his growing ardor and allow his good sense to prevail. Until he could know his own mind, Breck resolved to stay away from Nerissa Raleigh.

Chapter 14

It had been a stupid resolve. Breck recognized it as such within a very few minutes of leaving the Bridgewater theater box; for how, indeed, was he to distance himself from Nerissa when he had just committed to visiting her the very next afternoon?

He felt like an utter fool. When he felt foolish, he got angry, angry enough with himself to decide that he would not return to his seat to watch the rest of the opera. He could, he was sure, find better ways to pass his time than to sit through an opera performance, all the while fighting to keep his attention on the stage rather than on the other side of the theater, where Nerissa was seated.

"Give my regrets to your mother and father," he instructed Lord Crompton in a curt voice.

His lordship eyed him warily. He recognized the dark cloud of Breck's expression and debated for a moment the prudence of arguing with him. But the thought of the scold he would receive from his mother if he returned to their box without Breck prompted him to demand, "Don't tell me you are cutting out! Now? Why, the evening isn't even half over!"

"More the reason I should leave!" said Breck, and he called for his coat and hat. "I have stomached just about all the high-toned culture I can for one evening."

"Don't try to bamboozle me. I know you too well—well enough to know you like the opera!"

Breck cast him a devilishly pointed look. "Or perhaps I just like certain elements of it. Wave to the soprano for me, will you?"

He was out the door and on the street before his cousin could form a reply. He shrugged off the offer of a hackney, drew his coat about him, and set out to walk the short distance to his club. In the cold night air his pace was brisk and his stride long and purposeful, as if he could dispel all thoughts of Nerissa merely by walking away. But he arrived at Watier's still in a thunderous mood.

A few glasses of excellent brandy and a very decent game of cards at which he dropped a most sizable sum of money did little to improve his temper. At the card table he felt restless and unable to concentrate on the bids or the last turn of the dealer's hand. When he moved on to the subscription room, his dark and angry countenance warned all the other members in attendance against any thought of engaging him in conversation.

It was late indeed when he left the club and took once again to walking. A light snow had begun to fall, and the paving stones beneath his feet were slick, but he didn't slacken his pace.

He was making his way down St. James's Street when he spotted the Bridgewater barouche drawn up at the curb in front of the Hampden Club. The Hampden was an establishment as known for its distinguished membership and political conversations as Breck's own club was known for deep gaming and potent wines. He had never before set foot in the place, but he was seized with a sudden and keen desire to speak with Lord Arthur Bridgewater.

A steward greeted Breck and ushered him into the entry hall, where he invited Breck to wait while he announced his arrival to Lord Bridgewater. Only Hampden members, he informed Breck in an exalted tone, were allowed beyond the front room.

"No need. I won't be staying long. Just point me in the direction of Lord Bridgewater," said Breck with a darkling look that dared the steward to challenge him.

The steward debated for only a moment before he crossed the hall to open a heavy paneled door that gave off into a large subscription room. On the far side of the room, quite alone and seated in a comfortable chair by the window, was Arthur Bridgewater.

Arthur was not a man who regularly took to drink. He had, in fact, been in school the last time he had been on the toodle, but he was of the notion that it was high time he made up for it.

He had resolved to consume in a single evening the vast quantities of porter he was sure he had missed over the years. He was in possession of a tray of glasses and two full bottles of the stuff, and out of one he poured himself another drink. He was well on his way to being quite pleasantly foxed, when he chanced to look up to see Breck Davenant walking toward him down the length of the long room.

"Davenant? What brings you here? You're not a Hampden man!"

"Not by any stretch, I assure you," said Breck, laying off his coat and tossing it on a nearby chair with his hat and gloves. "I saw your carriage outside and the steward said I could find you here."

"I'm flattered. Join me in a glass of porter. Not as fine a wine as your cellars might produce, I dare say, but it's tolerable pleasant."

Breck accepted the glass from him and sat down. He gave Arthur a cursory examination and asked quite bluntly, "Well, are you drunk yet?"

Arthur's eyes widened for a moment, then he relaxed and smiled. "No. But I mean to be. Very shortly, as a matter of fact."

"Then I'm glad for the chance to speak to you before you drown your memory in porter fumes. I've come to talk to you about that sister-in-law of yours."

"Rissa? Why?" he asked warily. He had a sudden thought and blurted out, "Don't tell me she was following you on the streets again?"

Breck smiled slightly. "So you know about that, do you?"

"Of course! Anne was with her, you know. Of all the rackety ideas! I don't mind telling you that after their behavior, I was pretty surprised Rissa ever convinced you to agree to her scheme."

"So you know about that too. It was supposed to remain a secret between Nerissa and me."

"I'll never stain, so you needn't worry." Arthur eyed Breck measuringly for a moment. "Although I must admit, I've always been curious what on earth possessed you to agree to help such a foolishly romantic chit."

"That's what I wanted to talk to you about. You see, I've decided I won't be a party to Nerissa's plan any longer. I'd be obliged if you would tell her so for me."

Arthur eyed him suspiciously. "Tell Rissa you've decided to punt off? Why should I do that for you?"

"Because you're a decent man who doesn't lack for sense. Surely you know by my reputation I'm hardly a man who might ever be considered a suitable influence for the girl."

"Is that so? Well, as it happens, you're too late, Davenant. You see, I no longer have a bit of sense, nor do I care for suitable influences."

Breck watched Arthur throw back the last of the contents of his glass in a single, reckless gulp. "What do you mean?" he asked quietly.

"I mean I have learned at long last a most important lesson about women: they don't have the least interest in a good man. Oh, they say they do. They'll spend the better part of an entire afternoon cataloguing the virtues of the ideal male. But when it comes right down to the nib of the matter, women don't want anything to do with a man who is circumspect and loyal and who abides by a high code of ethics.''

"Is that so? It sounds as if you've given the matter a great deal of thought," said Breck. Up until then he hadn't realized just how much wine Arthur had consumed. He wasn't sure whether he should be amused or alarmed by the content or the thickness of his words. He asked most politely, "Tell me, then what *do* women want?"

"Bounders. Rogues. Men like—like you!" said Arthur, pointing a rather unfocused finger in Breck's direction.

"I see," said Breck, choosing his words with care. "Are you telling me that your wife—Lady Bridgewater—has formed an—an *attachment* for me?"

"Don't be daft. It isn't you!" said Arthur impatiently. "It's that cousin of yours. Don't think I haven't noticed the way she behaves whenever the cur is about, because I have."

"Crompton? You can't be serious. Listen to me a moment, Bridgewater—"

"Of course I'm serious! Not that anything untoward has yet occurred—at least I don't think so, at any rate. And I can hardly blame Anne. He's a dashed handsome fellow, you know—everyone in your family is! And he's probably twice as well-heeled as I am and many more times a better dancer—that sort of thing is very important to a woman."

"I see," said Breck. "It sounds as if you've given this matter quite a bit of thought."

"I'm not a fool," said Arthur with a penetrating look that belied his consumption of spirits. "I may not have heard what was being said between Anne and Crompton earlier tonight, but I've been blessed with more than competent eyesight. I know a flirtatious male eye when I see

one; likewise, a maidenly blush. There's something between them, mark me!''

"What,'' asked Breck in a cautious voice, ''do you intend
to do about it?''

"Fight. Oh, I don't mean to fight Crompton, so calm
yourself. I do mean, however, to fight to keep Anne. I
don't intend to just sit back and let her go quietly. It's a
hard thing to discover your wife is attracted to a man of
Crompton's ilk, and that a rogue can win her devotion.
But if a bounder and a rogue is what she wants, then—
then I guess I shall behave as one!''

"Is that why you're trying single-handedly to down the
better part of Hampden's wine reserve?'' asked Breck,
helping himself to another glass. "So you can gather
enough Dutch courage to abandon your usual principles?''

"Joke if you like,'' said Arthur sharply, "but know that
I am prepared to do whatever is necessary to keep my wife
out of your cousin's arms.''

"Bridgewater, listen to me. You have nothing to fear.
Your wife is not interested in a—a *dalliance* with my cousin!
Trust me on this!''

Arthur let out a hoot. "Trust *you?* Why should I, when
I know perfectly well you're the cause of this whole ghastly
mess!''

"Me?'' repeated Breck, his hand stopping in midair as
he lifted his glass to his lips. "What have I done, if you
don't mind my asking?

"You struck a bargain with my sister-in-law! You filled
Rissa's head with nonsense of heroes and swords and duels.
Before you entered our lives, Anne was quite happy to be
a simple politician's wife. Then you came along and Rissa
and Anne have been conspiring and dreaming of heroes
ever since! A fellow like me can never measure up to such
mummery!''

Breck swallowed the contents of his glass in one movement, just as he had seen Arthur do but moments before.
"This hero business,'' he said grimly, "has become nothing

more than some curst sword of Damocles hanging over my head!''

"If you don't mind my saying, I can't see what you've got to complain about. Every woman in London is on the scramble for you, and the two women I have to live with look up to you as if you were some sort of god!''

Breck felt his temper mount slightly. "But I'm not a god,'' he said impatiently, "nor am I a hero. I'm just a man, and I would like your sister-in-law to see me so just once!''

"So that's why you don't want to see Rissa again,'' said Arthur with a sudden, thoughtful frown. "You think she's interested in you only as a subject of literary research. You think she has no feelings for you as a man—for yourself.''

Breck opened his mouth to reply, a protest formed and ready on his lips. But he stopped and favored Arthur with a hard stare. "Tell me, are you always so sharp whenever you drink yourself into a stupor?''

Arthur responded with a loopy grin. "Sometimes I surprise even myself. I'd wager you're probably in love with her.''

"You'd lose,'' said Breck in a suddenly warning tone.

"She's probably in love with you too,'' pursued Arthur defiantly. "She'll never admit it though, because she's afraid of being leg-shackled to a husband who doesn't love her back.''

"She had that from her sisters,'' said Breck grimly, "and from a mother with more ambition than sense when it came time to marry off her daughters.''

"Yes, her sisters made some very unkind matches, I can tell you. Not a one of them is happy or loved.''

"Except for Anne,'' said Breck pointedly.

"Now who's sharp? I suppose I might as well admit it, since we're both being rather candid and nothing we say tonight will see the light of day. Yes, I love Anne. I've loved her since the moment I first met her. I knew she didn't want to marry me—thought I was dull!—but I decided that if I were kind to her and treated her with gentleness, she would come to love me one day."

"And you don't think that has happened?"

"Not yet and perhaps it never will. But if I can't have her love me, I might be able to make her proud of me and of the work I do in the Lords. If I can't be dashing in her eyes, perhaps she'll love me for being successful. Sometimes I think if I could only get my Corn Bill passed, she would think better of me."

"So get it passed," said Breck simply.

Arthur laughed. "You know less of politics than does my wife, Davenant! Getting a bill passed is not as simple as you make it sound, especially when Lord Kendrew has used his influence to block it at every turn!"

"My uncle? Why would he do that?"

"Partly to spite me. Partly because he sees no benefit for himself in passing it. I've tried to reason with him, but he won't budge."

"He'd budge if my brother Simon spoke to him," said Breck, pouring out another round from the bottle.

"The marquess? Do you think—Oh, but he's not interested—I could never get an audience—"

"No, but I could. I'll mention it to Simon the next time I see him."

"You'd do that for me?" asked Arthur, dazzled yet doubtful.

"If I remember. No promises, now!"

"That's very decent of you, Davenant. Very decent indeed. You're not as bad a chap as you would have everyone believe, are you?"

Was he? There was a time when Breck Davenant wouldn't have so much as lifted his quizzing glass in the direction of a man of Arthur Bridgewater's ilk. Yet there he sat, in a club of political leanings, speaking of corn bills and marriage, making promises and practically professing his love for a hurly-burly young woman who insisted she wanted nothing to do with him once she was through examining him like a bug under glass.

He had been accused so many times of being selfish and jaded that to have someone describe him as otherwise was something of a shock. Anything Arthur had to say after that stunning pronouncement went virtually unheard; and Breck was hardly aware when he made his good-byes and left the Hampden.

He walked home in that late winter night, feeling the sting of the snow on his face. Once again did he wrestle with a feeling of foolish disquiet; once again did he lay at Nerissa's door the blame for that unaccustomed feeling. The deuce of it was that the more he saw of her, the more his amusement over her antics gave way to a more tender sentiment. Contrary to what Arthur had said, he didn't think he was under love's spell. But Arthur had been correct on one point: Breck did want Nerissa to see him as a man. For some reason, it had grown important to Breck that Nerissa recognize his own worth, that she see him for himself and not as some model for a preposterous fictional character.

Why Nerissa's opinion of him should carry so much weight he couldn't say, for she wasn't at all like any of the other women with whom he had associated in the past. She was merely pretty rather than beautiful, managing instead of compliant. She was absurdly optimistic and relentlessly romantic, and, now that he came to consider it, he realized what a truly innocent sort of female she really was. In short, she was not at all the kind of woman who might have attracted his attention in the past. So why the devil did he find himself thinking of her so much?

For he did, indeed, think of her often, and he was more and more aware of a wish to shield her and protect her from the follies of her own enthusiasms.

Yet in Nerissa's words and demeanor, he could detect no similar sentiments on her part. She didn't at all behave as a woman who was the least attracted to him. It was a lowering thought. Barring those absurdly admiring looks she cast him, he didn't think she considered him anything more than a research subject to be observed, prodded, and examined.

That old anger born of foolishness quickened his step, and when at last he arrived home to find Henry waiting for him, he shunned Henry's assistance and put himself to bed. Sleep proved elusive and rest was out of the question. By the time the morning dawned snowing and bitterly cold, his mood had darkened considerably.

Breck considered canceling his drive out with Nerissa, but that notion was banished as quickly as it was formed. He wanted to see her. He *needed* to see her; he needed to hear her say in her own words what, if anything, she felt for him.

He had never before found himself in the dubious position of not knowing exactly how to go on with a woman. In all his previous dealings with the fairer sex, his courtships had been calculating and he had piped the tune. But with Nerissa he felt somehow out of his element. Because he couldn't be sure of her feelings, he wasn't sure of his own.

The thought occurred to him that he could very easily force her to declare herself, that it would take very little effort on his part to clasp her in his arms and kiss her until she confessed that she loved him. While he didn't think he would have need of such a drastic measure—pleasurable as it might prove to be—he did resolve to find out exactly what course her feelings had taken.

He arrived at Bridgewater House and was ushered into the drawing room to find Nerissa sitting prettily in wait for him. She stood and dipped a small curtsy accompanied by a beguiling smile. She was happy to see him again, for it was their first opportunity to be together since their ride in the hansom cab. They had spoken briefly at the theater, but with other patrons about them, she knew he had held himself in check, and there had been no opportunity for

them to converse in the companionable way they had
grown to do.

One glance up into Breck's tanned countenance, however, and Nerissa's level of happiness dropped a peg. He
was looking rather tight about the mouth, and he appeared
to be in one of his inaccessible moods. Truly, he didn't
look the least bit happy to see her. Her defenses instinc-
tively went up.

He didn't speak immediately, but waited for Nerissa to
be seated by the fire, then he claimed a chair pulled up
on the other side of the hearth.

"I think it a good idea to postpone our drive out for
another day," he said. "The weather has gone bad and
the roads have turned dangerous, I think."

Nerissa glanced out the window and saw that the snowfall
had increased. "Oh, dear, and I was so relying upon driving
out with you! You won't forget, will you, to take me another
day?"

"I won't forget," he said.

"Good, for I very much enjoy our drives. I have yet to
see another man in London who can control a pair of
horses with as much dash as you!"

One of his brows went up challengingly. "You mean
with as much dash as a hero, don't you?"

It was an odd question, and she didn't quite know what
to make of it. "Of course! Yes, that's exactly what I meant."

"But I'm *not* a hero," he said. "I'm just a man, Nerissa.
Your optimism and overinflated sense of romance have
blinded you, I think, to who I really am."

"Not at all! I know exactly who you are, for my sister
told me all about you!"

"Is that so? Then, where is your sister, Nerissa? If you
know all about me and what a rascal I am, don't you think
she should be present when I visit you?"

She was a little surprised to be asked such a question by
a man with whom she was so oftentimes alone. She said
in a tone of mild surprise, "She's with Arthur right now.

He came home quite late last night and has been ill all morning. I think my sister is nursing him."

Since Breck was himself a veteran of many late-night porter sprees, he wasn't at all surprised to hear of Arthur's condition. "That's an admirable thing for her to do, considering the fact that she's nursing a man she doesn't love."

Nerissa frowned. "How would you know what feelings my sister has?"

"You've told me of them often enough, haven't you? You've mentioned all your sisters and their marriages on more than one occasion, I think."

He was speaking quietly, concealing all trace of emotion in his voice. It was not an easy task for him, for no sooner had he entered the drawing room and seen Nerissa standing in front of that impossibly adorned Christmas tree than he had felt suddenly and irrationally overjoyed to see her. For a brief moment he had thought he had detected the same look of happiness on her face. Then he had seen her expression fall, and he knew that her sentiments did not match his own. In an instant he had felt resentful and rather abominably used. He was having a devil of a time keeping his temper under control.

His feelings upon seeing her again had startled him. When he suddenly recalled that Arthur Bridgewater had accused him of being in love with Nerissa, he resolved to double his efforts to hide all trace of emotion until he could better gauge what was in her heart.

He did a good job of it, for Nerissa could tell nothing of the thoughts parading through his mind. But she could tell Breck seemed a bit out of sorts and rather irrational—traits that were not at all of his usual mien. "Would you rather I didn't speak of my sisters?" she asked in some perplexity. "Would you rather I didn't hold them up as examples of what the future might hold for me?"

He directed a very penetrating look upon her. "I'm well aware of your sisters and their plights. I'd rather you spoke only of yourself, frankly."

"Very well," said Nerissa, searching for some neutral topic of conversation. She brightened suddenly and said, "I believe I have finished my book at long last. I sent a card around to Mr. Heble, the publisher, to tell him I shall call upon him on Christmas Eve to deliver it. I—I hope you will wish me well!"

"Is that still your aim, Nerissa?" asked Breck with a flinty look to his eye. "Do you still intend to publish your book? Do you still mean to harden your heart against marriage?"

"Harden my heart? No such thing, I assure you!" she said with a slight laugh.

He frowned. "What's so funny?"

"You! One minute you are chiding me for being romantic and optimistic, and the next moment you take me to task for merely being practical!"

His dark brows rose. "Practical? You call writing a romantic novel practical?"

"If I don't want to marry," she said very patiently, "I must have a means of supporting myself. I must have my book published."

"But why couldn't you marry?" he countered. "You could stay on in London with your sister and be presented in the new year. You might find by then that your sentiments have changed. You might find you've fallen in love with a man."

She shook her head slightly. "That is exactly what I wish to avoid." She could have said more. She could have told Breck that falling in love with a man and not being loved in return was probably her very greatest fear. And she had come to realize, just within the past few days, how great a fear it truly was.

Aside from their brief encounter at the theater, she hadn't seen Breck in days. She had missed him, she had longed for him, and her need for him had proved to be as unwelcome as it was surprising for her. She had thought to have protected her heart very well against his charms, and it was a hard thing to admit that despite her best efforts, she was well on her way to falling desperately in love with Breck Davenant.

It was her worse nightmare realized, for it was quite obvious to Nerissa that Breck did not return her regard. If he cared for her at all, she thought, he would take her in his arms and kiss her, as she had once asked him to do. Instead, he sat quite languidly on the other side of the hearth, looking back at her with a dark expression that was nothing short of forbidding.

"You're woefully innocent, Nerissa, about a good many things," he said in a quietly controlled voice. "Most important, you're wrong to think that married couples cannot love each other."

Her chin went up a notch. "Is that so? Offhand, I cannot think of anyone who is happily married, can you?"

"Yes, as a matter of fact I can! My own family, for one! My brothers and sisters, and aunts and uncles—all happily married and all quite in love with their mates."

"Indeed? If their marriages are such pattern cards of perfection, how is it that *you* have not followed their examples?" she asked rather defensively.

"Me? There are a good many reasons, I dare say. Perhaps I have just never yet met a woman I would marry," he said, his gaze never wavering from her face.

In fact, he was looking at her so intently, she thought he could not possibly miss the fact that her eyes had gone wide with shock. Those simple words, which he had uttered with such callousness, held the same effect as a pail of cold water being dashed in her face.

She was on her feet in an instant, her fingers gripped very tightly together in an effort to control her flying emotions.

"The same, I assure you, might be said of me," she answered in a tight little voice. "Perhaps I have never met a man *I* would wish to marry."

Breck rose too, slowly and rather ominously. While his gaze remained on her face, his dark brows had knit together and his pale eyes had narrowed somewhat.

He had never seen Nerissa's temper before, and he was unsure how to go on or how far to push her. "Are you telling me the truth?" he asked slowly. "Can you honestly say to me that you have no feeling—no affection—" He stopped short, aware that he had verged on revealing what was in his heart.

He needn't have worried, for Nerissa had been so stunned by his first pronouncement, she was barely aware of what had followed. She knew only that she was deeply hurt by the words he had blurted out, and she said, falsely bright, "No, indeed! Goodness, what kind of a chucklehead should I be to allow myself to be presented in the new year, knowing very well I could never marry *any* man! No, thank you! I shall stick to my original plan and finish my days more the happier for it, I think. If my book does prove to be a success, I shall have you to thank. You've been a tremendous help to me, and you may consider your promise kept, your obligation to me fulfilled!"

Breck's eyes narrowed more. "Is that all you can think to say to me: thank you, and good-bye?"

The door to the drawing room opened and Anne entered. "Oh, Rissa, Arthur is still too ill to go out this evening—" She stopped short, a little surprised by the face-off before her. "Why, Mr. Davenant, I didn't know you were already come to take my sister driving!"

"We won't be driving out after all," said Nerissa, carefully keeping her voice even. "The weather has turned, you see, and—and Mr. Davenant was just now leaving!"

Anne looked from Nerissa to Breck and back again. She went to Breck with her hand outstretched. "Were you?

Then I am glad for the chance to see you before you whisk yourself away."

"You must say your good-byes to Mr. Davenant, Anne," said Nerissa quite ruthlessly. "You see, I have no more need of Mr. Davenant, nor he of me! I dare say we shall never have occasion to see him again!"

Chapter 15

Breck Davenant had been thrown out of ladies' drawing rooms before—usually by irate husbands but never by innocent maids. It was a new experience for him to be dismissed so ruthlessly by a woman to whom he was very close to declaring himself. The experience did not sit well.

He swung his tall, muscular body up into his curricle and set off down the icy street at a pace that sent the snow pelting against his face and caused Henry to grip the sides of the seat with more than usual vigor.

He was driving past Grosvenor Square, still in a dark mood, when he saw drawn before his brother's house several traveling chaises, each bearing the Davenant coat of arms. A closer inspection revealed that while the standard of the marquessate had not been set to flying, the knocker had been mounted upon the door and there was a distinct bustle of activity on the street and walkway in front of the house.

Breck frowned and slowed his horses. "Henry, have I had a letter from my brother recently?"

"No, sir."

"My sister-in-law?"

"Not that I know, Mr. Breck," said Henry, drawing on his memory. "If one of them was to write saying they were coming to town, I think you would have remembered."

"As do I," said Breck, setting his curricle in motion again. "Well, something's amiss to have brought my brother Simon and his family to London three days before Christmas. Now the only question remains whether I am of a curious enough nature to find out what it is."

He decided that question by drawing in behind one of the chaises and handing the reins to Henry. Mounting the front steps two at a time, Breck entered the house to find the center hall littered with trunks and bandboxes, portmanteaux and bundles of linens. Three footmen, two maids, and a butler were scurrying about under the direction of a petite, middle-aged woman still garbed in traveling dress. Breck rapped lightly upon the hall table, and she spun about, breaking off, in midsentence, the last of a list of instructions to the servants.

"Why, Breck! What a pleasure," she said, going to him immediately with her hands outstretched.

He kissed his sister-in-law's cheek and said politely, "Jane! I wish you and my brother had let me know you were come to town."

"Oh, Simon isn't here yet, and I arrived only just now, in fact not above ten minutes ago," said the marchioness. "Simon will be here tomorrow and the children the day after. I came ahead to set the house to rights and ready the rooms. After all, if we are to spend Christmas in London—as I told your brother, most firmly—we simply must have everything the very same as if we were celebrating at home at Pankhurst Castle!"

"Christmas in London?" repeated Breck. "Is that your intention? Why?"

In the face of this blunt question, Lady Pankhurst looked up at him and smiled. "Well, I shall tell you. Only come into the drawing room, if you please! I'm eager to lay off my things and make myself a little comfortable.''

She instructed the butler to bring in a tray of refreshments and sailed into the drawing room with all the grace and elegance for which she was famed. She removed her gloves and hat, followed by her pelisse and settled herself comfortably upon a chair by the fire before she directed her clear hazel eyes upon him.

Breck had moved away to remove his own driving coat and hat, and as he turned back toward her, he carelessly tossed those items upon a nearby chair. Lady Pankhurst's interest quickened. The gesture, she knew, was uncharacteristic. The Breck Davenant of her ken would no more consider tossing his clothing onto a chair than he would consider tossing them into the Thames.

She didn't realize she had been staring up at him until Breck claimed the chair opposite her and asked, ''What is it? Why do you look at me so?''

She clasped her hands together in her lap and forced a light note to her voice. ''I was thinking just now how very smart you are. I wish you'd take your brother in hand while he's here. Simon hasn't had a new coat in ages, and his sense of style has depreciated to that of a country squire. He could stand a bit of your polish.''

''He could stand to lose a bit of weight,'' said Breck dryly. ''I don't suppose he's done so?''

Lady Pankhurst shook her head and laughed. ''It's that country living. Simon enjoys our time at Pankhurst Castle more with every passing year.''

''In that case, I think I won't introduce him to my tailor, if it's all the same. I have a reputation to maintain, you know.''

He watched Jane laugh softly as he leaned back a bit into the comfort of his chair. Of all his relations, Breck liked Jane the most. She had been married to his eldest brother just over eighteen years, and he had counted her, from to time, as something of a friend as well as a sister-in-law.

Jane was the only member of the Davenant family who had never tried to ply her wiles, persuasions, and arguments against him. To his memory, she had never attempted to conform him to any family protocol or lecture him over his refusal to behave as befitting the noble house of Davenant.

Yes, he liked Jane very well. She was a lovely woman of breeding and style, an excellent wife, and a stunning marchioness. Affection aside, he didn't for a moment believe she had come all the way to London in the middle of a winter snowstorm merely to celebrate the Christmas holiday.

He scanned her sunny face and said, "And you, Jane? How do you go on? Never mind—no need to tell me! You're looking well. Well enough for me to think you didn't make the trip for reasons of health. So tell me: just why *are* you come to London?"

She cocked a brow and smiled at him. "I shall take that as a compliment, if you don't mind. And I thought I already answered your question. I've come to spend the holiday here."

"You've never spent Christmas at any other but Pankhurst Castle with your children about you. Why the change this year, if you don't mind my asking?"

"Not at all," she answered smoothly. "I've decided to spend Christmas in London so you would not be alone."

That surprised him into a moment's silence. "Did it never occur to you that I prefer to be alone at Christmas? Every year you and my brother invite me to stay with you at Pankhurst—"

"And every year you decline the invitation. Yes, I know! But this year is different."

"How so?" he asked politely.

She started to answer him but stopped when the door to the drawing room opened and her butler appeared with a tray of refreshments. When she was done directing its placement and turned back toward Breck, she saw that his attention had wandered to the decorative carvings on the lip of a nearby table. She watched him unconsciously reach over to trace the intricate design with his fingertip.

"I have had a letter from your aunt Kendrew," she said slowly with an eye to his still-roving finger. "She wrote a very pretty invitation to me. She deplores the distance that has grown within our family and looks to Simon and me to do a bit of reconciling among relatives. I believe she was particularly concerned about you."

That brought his head up. "*Me?* You mistake, my dear. The only time my aunt Kendrew is the least interested in me is when I receive an invitation to a *tonnish* affair and she does not!"

"*I* took her letter seriously," said Jane, ignoring the truth of his statement, "and I agree with her that there has been some change in you since last I saw you."

"Nonsense," he replied with a smile of great sweetness. "And you shall soon see for yourself that I am every bit as selfish, provoking, and unprincipled as I ever was."

She laughed. "There are reports to the contrary, I assure you!"

"So you've come to see for yourself whether it's true? Well, have a look," he said, standing and inviting her to examine his person. "Am I or am I not the very same hooligan who has long been the scourge of the Davenant family?"

"No more of your nonsense, if you please," said Jane through a barely disguised smile. "And since you take so much pride in your reputation as a hooligan, you'll be pleased to know your aunt Kendrew still believes you to be one."

"A circumstance I find most gratifying."

Jane thought he would say more, but he didn't. Instead, he moved off and began to travel the room rather absently. At a side table he picked up a knickknack, then set it down after barely looking at it. At the mantel shelf he did the same with a candlestick, and at the window he twitched impatiently at the draperies.

She recognized uncommon behavior in her brother-in-law when she saw it, and asked rather gently, "Breck, is anything amiss?"

"I shouldn't think so. Why?"

"I think," she said slowly, "your aunt Kendrew may be right."

"Indeed?" he asked expectantly. When he saw Jane catch her lower lip between her even white teeth, he frowned. "Just what, exactly, did my aunt Kendrew write?"

"Breck, she writes that you have formed a—a mésalliance!" she said in a rush. "Oh, dear, I didn't say that with the least delicacy! Breck, I *am* sorry! But your aunt Kendrew is very concerned and wrote to your brother and me only out of affection, I am sure!"

"So my brother coerced you into coming ahead to find out if the on-dit is true, eh?"

"Not at all! I volunteered."

Breck moved slowly toward the fireplace and took a moment to gaze down into the dancing flames. This was a turn he had not expected. He had been so sure that he had behaved with great care where Nerissa was concerned. Aside from their occasional drives out, he had taken great pains to ensure that he was seen with Anne and Arthur just as much as he was with Nerissa. He had thought he had routed the tattle-mongers. Apparently, he was wrong.

He knew his aunt Kendrew to be a woman of grossly underdeveloped powers of intuition. Yet if she were astute enough to have gauged what was in his heart, then he had misjudged his own behavior.

He looked up at Jane and said cautiously, "My aunt is, I think, rushing at the wrong fence. There is no mésalliance."

"She writes that you have been seen everywhere in her company," prompted Jane.

"Did she happen to write that the young lady in question is of suitable birth and charm?"

"No, but she did write that the girl is terribly young and not at all in your usual line. Breck, I'm afraid I must agree with your aunt: Anne Bridgewater is not for you."

He looked at her sharply and let out a sudden and bitter laugh. "Leave it to my aunt Kendrew to make a mull of it! Calm yourself, dear Jane. My interest does not run toward Lady Bridgewater."

"I'm glad to hear it," she said, relieved. "I'm not acquainted with Anne Bridgewater, but I have met her mother. Lady Raleigh is a foolish woman who raised five very foolish daughters, so I've been told. But I'm puzzled to think your aunt might have written otherwise. After all, it's not like her to be so very much off the mark where you're concerned. She's been too keen an observer of your behavior and much too jealous of you not to make it her business to know your every move."

He didn't respond immediately, but began to travel the room again. His movements were far from those of his habitual grace and his step was agitated, as if some force, unknown even to him, drove him on.

Jane watched him with a growing feeling of unease until she could no longer keep from blurting out, "Breck dear, are you quite well?"

He stopped and turned to cast her an unreadable look. "Why do you keep asking that?"

"Because you are hardly yourself—nor have you been since you arrived."

He straightened slightly and frowned. "I'm not the least different, that I'm aware."

"That's just the problem! You're *not* aware! You've been pacing this drawing room on the order of a caged animal. You're forgetful and inattentive. You're not yourself, Breck."

His frown grew. "What utter rot. You're exaggerating, I think."

"I don't think so," she said quietly, her gaze never wavering from his face.

He was silent a moment, then he reclaimed the chair opposite her and said rather slowly, "Perhaps you're right. I have been a bit . . . distracted." He offered her his most engaging smile. "Now that you mention it, I believe I have been *very* absentminded. This morning, for instance, I think—I could be wrong, mind you!—but I think I ordered the mantel to draw my bath and struck a match on Henry."

She laughed. "Make sport as you like, you wretched man, but you won't convince me otherwise. There *is* something amiss with you. Don't deny it! I've known you too well these years not to notice when you've taken a crack-brained start, as my eldest boy would say."

"You're very certain of yourself," he remarked.

"Certain enough to know that the change in you may not be due to Anne Bridgewater, but it is definitely due to a woman. Breck dear, are—are you in love?"

"Love? That's a very strong word, don't you think?"

"It is, but not *too* strong, I notice, or you would have denied it straightaway."

He cast her an odd little smile. "I think the foreign office could use you, Jane. You could interrogate prisoners and trick them into divulging their secrets."

"Wretch!" she accused, and laughed softly. "Now, be serious, do, and tell me the truth at long last."

He stood again, went to the fire, and gazed into the flames for a moment or two.

"Who is she?" Jane asked in a gentle voice. When she received no answer, she prompted, "You said she was charming. Do I know her?"

He looked up then. "I don't think so. She's Anne Bridgewater's younger sister, Nerissa."

"I see," said Jane knowingly. "That's why your aunt was thrown so far off the scent!"

"Exactly! No one knows better than my aunt Kendrew that schoolgirls are usually not at all in my style."

"And is that what troubles you so?" she asked kindly. "Are you worried that she is so young?"

He looked down upon her for a very long while, his eyes as hard as agates and just as unreadable. "She won't have me," he said at last in a voice so low, she thought for a moment she had misunderstood.

"Won't—won't have you? What utter nonsense! Breck, you cannot be serious!"

"I am most serious. She won't have me."

"But I don't understand!" said Lady Pankhurst, bewildered. "There isn't a woman in England who wouldn't throw her heart over the first jump if you so much as crooked your finger her direction. Why, it doesn't make sense!"

"It does to her. You see, she insists she doesn't want to marry any man. Even me."

"Well, that settles it!" said Lady Pankhurst in deep disgust. "I was inclined to think well of Miss Nerissa Raleigh, for your sake, but I can see now that the gossip about her and her sisters is quite on the mark. Every last one of them must be as daft as a brush, or the youngest of them wouldn't be caught spouting such utter nonsense!"

Breck shook his head. "It's not nonsense to Nerissa. To her, it makes perfect sense and, oddly enough, it does to me too."

"But, Breck, what does she mean by it? Why, I never heard of a young girl not wanting to marry and be loved!"

"But therein lies the problem. You see, Nerissa insists she has never known anyone to be truly happy in marriage. I don't suppose it ever occurred to her that love and marriage just might go hand in hand."

"With her mother and her sisters as examples, I shouldn't wonder that the poor girl is so confused. Lady Raleigh has been quite mercenary in launching her daughters down the aisle, I've been told."

"She'll have a difficult time launching this one," said Breck with the hint of a smile. "Nerissa is taking great steps to ensure she shall not be compelled to marry and suffer the same fate as her sisters." He gave a short, bitter laugh. "The damnable thing of it is that for all her rebellious words to the contrary, I know she cares for me!"

"Do you think so, Breck?" asked Lady Pankhurst, her interest piqued.

"I'm sure of it, in fact. But she refuses to contemplate marriage. She swears she has never known anyone to be happily married."

"Then perhaps she should be introduced to your family. You're the youngest of eleven children, and every blessed one of them is quite happily situated in marriage—except, of course, for you! Why even your aunt Kendrew—for all the troubles and jealousies she stirs—has been blissfully married to her lord and master a good many years longer than I've been married to Simon."

"True and I mentioned that to her, but I don't think she believed me."

"*Make* her believe you!"

He cocked a challenging brow. "How?"

"Leave it to me! Oh, don't look so alarmed! I shan't give you away, you know! I shall simply send a card, asking her to visit—tomorrow, perhaps, once Simon is here. I confess, I'm rather eager to meet her. And I should think that between Simon and me and the rest of your brothers and sisters, we might contrive to make Miss Nerissa Raleigh witness for herself some most happily married couples."

Chapter 16

The invitation bearing the signature of the marchioness arrived while Nerissa was still in her room, putting the finishing touches to her morning *toilette*. The maid who delivered the missive bore it reverently upon a silver salver and informed her mistress that a footman, dressed in a very elegant livery, had brought it but moments before with the request that the letter be delivered to Miss Raleigh with all possible speed.

Nerissa didn't recognize the hand, but she did recognize the quality of the embossed writing paper and tore it open immediately. Her attention was caught by the signature: *Jane Pankhurst.* For a moment she thought there had been some mistake, that a letter intended for some highborn lady of fashion had somehow been delivered to the wrong house. But when she reread the first line and saw that the note was definitely addressed to her, Nerissa lost no time in reading the few simple sentences. She was even more puzzled after mastering the contents of the letter.

She went in search of Anne and found her still at late

breakfast with Arthur. Nerissa thrust the note at her and watched Anne's eyes widen slightly.

She allowed her sister a moment to read it and demanded, "Tell me what this means!"

"Good heavens!" breathed Anne as she handed the letter across to her husband. "You've been invited to visit the marchioness!"

"There—there must be some mistake," said Nerissa as she awaited Arthur's reaction.

"No, the note is very clear," he said, having scanned the few brief sentences. "You're to go this afternoon."

"By all that's wonderful, this is an honor!" said Anne, her eyes sparking. "Arthur, we must have the barouche. And, Rissa dear, you must wear your blue pelisse with the sable muff and bonnet to match. I shall wear my green, I think, unless, dear Rissa, you think it shall clash with your blue."

Arthur frowned. "Just a moment, Anne. The note is very specific: Rissa has been invited to go alone."

"Alone? Gracious, why would the marchioness wish to meet you alone, dear?"

"Truly, I can think of no reason," said Nerissa, but even as she said those words, she knew herself for a liar. She had a sudden and frightful notion that Lady Pankhurst had been told the tale of her trip to the Westminster Pit. Further reflection told her that it was unlikely Lady Pankhurst could have heard of her folly unless Breck had told her of it himself, and that prospect proved unlikely. Still, Nerissa couldn't be comfortable with the fact that she was being suddenly and unexpectedly singled out to receive her ladyship's attentions. To Nerissa's way of thinking, the invitation may have been prettily and kindly written, but guilt over her hoydenish behavior and a memory of Breck's coldness the last time they met combined to convince her to view the invitation at worst as something rather ominous, and at best, as nothing short of a summons for a scold.

She worked her hands together rather worriedly. "I—I don't think I can go. I think it would be best if I declined the invitation with thanks and with the deepest regret."

"Not go?" repeated Arthur.

"Rissa, what can you be thinking?" demanded Anne. "Of course you must go! When I think of the honor you have received to be singled out—why, I won't hear of such nonsense."

"But—but what about the weather?"

"The snow has stopped," said Arthur, "and while I don't doubt it's bitterly cold outside, you haven't that far to go to Pankhurst House."

Nerissa tried another tack. "But this has to be a mistake! Why would the marchioness ask me to wait upon her—*alone*?"

"Perhaps she means to take you up, Rissa dear," said Anne. "Oh, I do hope that's the case! Won't Lady Kendrew rust in the rain when she realizes she must recognize us after all!"

"If that were true, she would invite you, not me," said Nerissa. She turned beseeching eyes upon her brother-in-law. "Arthur, you're a reasonable man who cares nothing for society or fashion. Don't you think it a bit curious—"

"I see nothing curious about it at all," he said, a good deal shocked. "Of course you must go! If, by chance, you are introduced to the marquess, I hope you will do me the favor of mentioning my name. Tell him for me that I may be young, but my work is no less important because of it. Mention that I have spoken at length to Mr. Davenant about a certain bill I've been pushing to get passed. Do you think you can remember that?"

She didn't think she would be able even to remember her own name, so nervous was she as she went back upstairs to change her dress and prepare to visit Lady Pankhurst. She dawdled as long as possible and kept the barouche and horses waiting in the cold many more minutes while she made several trips back up to her room. The first delay was to collect a forgotten handkerchief; the second was due to a missing vial of hartshorn; and yet a third time did she return to her room to change her gloves after Anne had detected a small spot on the pair she was wearing.

It was rather late in the afternoon when at last she was ushered into the front hall at Pankhurst House. A very stately butler conducted her up to her ladyship's drawing room, and when the door was flung open and her name announced, Nerissa had to force herself to step across the threshold. The door closed behind her, but instead of walking farther into the room, she stood frozen to the spot.

Her cheeks went scarlet, and in the depths of her sable muff her hands clasped together tightly. She had thought her audience with the marchioness would be private and quite confidential, but there had to be at least six or seven very elegant-looking people in the room, all standing close by the fire, and all dressed in warm traveling clothes. If she was not mistaken, a good many of them bore a very striking resemblance to Breck Davenant.

Breck himself was at the window, and Nerissa had no doubt he had watched her approach from the street. He made no move toward her, and she could detect no greeting or welcome in his even, bland expression.

Lady Pankhurst left the clutch of people by the hearth and came forward, her hand outstretched and a smile of welcome on her lips. "Ah, Miss Raleigh," she said, "how brave of you to come to me in the face of such atrociously cold weather. I had quite given up on you—indeed, I wouldn't have thought any less if you had declined my invitation and stayed cozy and warm at home."

Nerissa dipped a curtsy and quite heartily wished she had done just so. She cast a worried look up into the sunny face of her hostess. "I'm very sorry to call so late and to have kept you waiting. Shall—shall I go? I wouldn't want to intrude upon your guests!"

"Not at all! You've come upon a mere family gather-

ing—we stand on no ceremony here! Come over by the
fire and let me introduce you, my dear.''

The next few moments were very much a blur to Nerissa.
She recalled meeting Lord Pankhurst, a handsome gentleman of middle age who, except for his advanced years and
heavier weight, might have been mistaken for Breck's twin.
She had made a deep curtsy before him and breathed a
sigh of relief that she hadn't humiliated herself with a
wobble. She was next very prettily presented to the other
occupants of the room, who, as she had suspected, were
each related to Breck either by blood or marriage.

Throughout all the introductions she remained burningly aware of Breck's presence by the window and of his
pale gray eyes watching her every move. Lady Pankhurst
acknowledged him with only a passing wave of her hand,
saying, ''You are acquainted already with my brother-in-
law, I believe. Now, my dear, what do you think? There's
a very prettyish wood just outside Berkhampstead, and not
a moment before you arrived we were thinking to drive
there to collect our sprigs and bowers and garlands.''

Nerissa looked at her blankly. ''Why do you want to do
that?''

''Tomorrow is Christmas Eve, my dear, and we must
make the house ready,'' said her ladyship.

''But—but won't you have your servants do that for
you?''

''Gracious, no! Decorating the house is something the
family does together. If the children were here, they would
help as well, but they won't arrive until tomorrow, bless
them. We adults shall just have to gather everything we
need on our own. Now, my dear, say you will come with
us! I won't take no for an answer!''

Nerissa cast a doubtful look about her. ''I wouldn't want
to *intrude* in any way . . .''

Lord Pankhurst was drawing on his gloves, and at this
he stopped and threw Nerissa a slight smile. ''Nonsense,
Miss Raleigh,'' he said in a deep, rumbling voice. ''You

won't be intruding at all. You'll ride with Lady Pankhurst and me, of course!''

There were no more protests to be made. Nerissa submitted to joining the party and climbed aboard a very comfortable landaulet along with Lord and Lady Pankhurst. There was plenty of room to be had in the carriage, and additional passengers might have joined them and been seated quite comfortably, but no one else made a move to travel with Nerissa and the Pankhursts. The rest of the family members, including Breck, who cast one last glance over his shoulder in Nerissa's direction, sorted themselves into the two other conveyances waiting at the curb.

With a fourth and last vehicle filled with servants, they set off in a caravan for Berkhampstead. Nerissa did her best to make conversation with Lord and Lady Pankhurst, but she was far from easy and could not be comfortable no matter how gracious and charming a host and hostess they appeared to be—and they appeared to be very amiable indeed. They were attentive and very kind and, as Nerissa observed, they were quite happy with their situation in life.

Once while they were traveling, Nerissa's attention was caught by a slight movement, and she saw that Lord Pankhurst had clasped his wife's hand and held it for a few moments. Then they had exchanged a look that, though brief, held a wealth of tender affection.

Nerissa recalled that Breck had mentioned that his brothers and sisters were all very happily married. Certainly, Lord and Lady Pankhurst matched that description very nicely. They were devoted to each other and, if that look they had exchanged were anything to be judged, they were in love with each other too.

At a staging inn at Watford they left the carriages and climbed into large, open, horse-drawn sleighs that would more easily travel off the road and over the fields toward the wood. Once again Nerissa was the only passenger to travel with Lord and Lady Pankhurst. With a fur carpet across her lap and a warm brick at her feet, Nerissa felt a bit more comfortable in their presence and was able to respond not quite as breathlessly whenever Lady Pankhurst made a comment or posed a question.

"My dear, I hope you'll help us gather everything we shall need to decorate the house. We're dreadfully tardy in making this trip, but I arrived in London only yesterday and Simon arrived just this morning. No doubt, Bridgewater House has already been decorated quite nicely."

Nerissa shook her head. "My sister, Anne, says we mustn't decorate the house until Christmas Eve, for it is bad luck to do otherwise." She thought for a moment, then added helpfully, "But we do have a tree!"

"A tree?" asked Lady Pankhurst blankly.

"A Christmas tree. It's in our drawing room, decorated very beautifully with cloved apples and candles and bits of ribbons and brass."

"I see," said Lady Pankhurst, thinking that there must be more to the story than her young guest had yet divulged. "Why do you have a decorated tree in your drawing room?"

"It's a German tradition," explained Nerissa. "I was at a ball at the German Embassy and saw one in the family apartments. It was the most beautiful thing I had ever seen, so Breck gave me one."

"Breck gave you a *tree?*" demanded Lady Pankhurst.

"Oh, yes. He's forever doing one thoughtful thing or another for me. He even let me observe him so I might write about him as one of the characters in my book."

There was something rather artless in Nerissa's delivery of such a stunning disclosure. Lady Pankhurst was very fond of her brother-in-law, but that didn't mean she was blind to his faults. She had never before heard him described as being thoughtful, nor had she ever known him to be cooperative enough to allow a complete and total stranger to observe his behavior. She asked, delving to the roots, "And what character would that be, my dear?"

"The hero. Breck Davenant is the perfect model of a dashing hero. You must have noticed it before."

Lady Pankhurst didn't know whether to be shocked to silence or laugh aloud. She cast a look up at her husband's face and saw that he appeared to be just as bewildered by such innocent disclosures as she. "I have heard my brother-in-law described a good many ways," she said slowly, "but never as a hero!"

"Oh, but he is! Why, one of the first times I met him, he came to my rescue! He's just as dashing and compelling a figure when he's cutting out a dance partner as he is tooling his sporting curricle about town. Truly, everything about him is larger than life and twice as heroic!"

There was much for Lady Pankhurst to consider in these admiring words. That Nerissa Raleigh was young and hopelessly idealistic she could not doubt. What was even more intriguing, though, was that Nerissa's romantic optimism could not have been at greater odds with Breck's usual cynicism. If they were to make a match of it, she didn't think it would last; but then again, neither Nerissa nor Breck had thus far behaved at all as one would expect. If Lady Pankhurst was not mistaken, it was probably Nerissa's unwavering admiration that had attracted Breck in the first place, and since Nerissa had firmly believed him to be the embodiment of a true hero, he had responded by behaving as one. Truly, Breck Davenant could do worse than to fall in love with a woman who idolized him.

Judging from the spark of affection in Miss Raleigh's eyes and the faint tinge of color that touched her cheeks whenever Breck's name was mentioned, Lady Pankhurst rather suspected that Nerissa felt very much the same way about him. All that remained, she decided, was that Nerissa should be brought to change her mind about marriage— that and a little bit of time alone together, she thought, should do the trick and tie the whole affair up nicely.

They arrived at the sparsely wooded countryside outside Berkhampstead. Lady Pankhurst immediately began to direct everyone in the proper way to hunt for pine branches, holly, and ivy.

"Miss Raleigh," she said with a slight gesture to where Breck was standing, "you must allow my brother-in-law to escort you. A servant will follow to gather up any of the boughs and branches you choose. Breck has done this before and can show you the way—you'll be quite comfortable with him!"

Nothing could have been further from the truth. Nerissa felt her cheeks color with a recollection of everything that had passed between them the last time they met. She couldn't be sure if Breck was thinking the very same thing, and she glanced quickly up into his face. His mouth was drawn into a very inviting smile, his brows were lifted slightly, and there was a question in his eyes. Besides that quizzing look, in the depths of his pale eyes she saw a very disturbing expression.

"Anyone can collect pine boughs," he said, clasping her elbow and propelling her away from family and servants and toward a grove of junipers. "Let us find something a little different to take back to the house."

Even through the thick material of her pelisse, Nerissa was burningly aware of his touch at her elbow. She had little choice but to walk where he led, but she said rather discouragingly, "I think I've had enough of your new ideas for Christmas. I told Lady Pankhurst about our Christmas tree and I thought the poor woman would fall off her seat! She did her very best not to laugh aloud, but I could tell she wanted to! If it's all the same to you, I don't think I care to tempt her again."

His brow went up. "Don't you like the Christmas tree any longer?"

"Of course I like it! It's beautiful, but . . ."

"And of all the things I've taught you and all the new experiences I've introduced you to in the past few weeks, you haven't yet been disappointed, have you?" he asked, drawing her inexorably on toward the trees.

"Not at all! But my book is complete and I can think of nothing else you might need to show me!"

"Only this," he said, coming to an abrupt halt and pulling her unceremoniously into his arms. His lips were on hers before she could think or utter a shadow of a protest. But after a very short moment, protesting was the last thing on her mind. His lips teased hers with a practiced expertise that left her feeling as if she had had an electric shock. A sudden warmth danced to life within her, and she felt a trifle dizzy. By the time he raised his head and looked down upon her, she was unabashedly clinging to the lapels of his cloak and hoping with all her being that he would kiss her some more.

He smiled slightly and said in a tone that was somewhat deeper than his usual voice, "You've just sampled yet another Christmas tradition, my innocent: kissing under the mistletoe."

She looked up then, and saw that they were indeed standing just beneath a juniper tree, its branches woven with mistletoe. "You knew!" she said, sounding more joyous than severe. "You lured me to this place!"

"I would have dragged you if I had to. I should have kissed you long ago, when I first had the chance. Little did I know then what pleasure I was missing."

"I think perhaps we should take some mistletoe back with us, then," she said, smiling up at him in a manner that was at once provocative and shy. "We could make it up into several different kissing boughs and position them in every doorway throughout the house."

"Or better still, I might just take a ribbon and tie a sprig in your hair. But I warn you: then you shall find me kissing you day and night."

He tightened his arms about her and lowered his lips once more toward hers. He wasn't quite sure which he found more enticing, the innocent abandon with which she returned his embrace or the fact that her responding kiss convinced him, as nothing else could, that she did indeed care for him. In that kiss, Breck knew that Nerissa's resolve to remain unmarried was only so much posturing. She did care for him, he was sure. With that assurance came an even stronger determination that she should abandon her plan to earn her own living and live instead with him as his wife.

When at last he raised his head, Nerissa looked up into his eyes with a radiant expression. "Did—did you mean what you just said?" she asked rather tentatively.

"About kissing you day and night? Of course!"

"Breck, are—are you asking me to *marry* you?"

"Yes, my innocent, I *am!* Well, *will* you marry me? Say, yes, drat you!"

She was half afraid she might burst with happiness. Almost, she said yes; almost, she abandoned all the plans and principles she had formed about marriage. But some unknown scruple caused her to hesitate and say instead, "I shall give you an answer presently, but first, Breck, isn't there something you have forgot to mention?"

"Never fear," he said, planting a silky kiss upon her forehead. "As your husband, I won't curb your affairs— you may scribble your books to your heart's content!"

Those were not at all the words she had been waiting to hear. Her level of happiness dropped a peg. "And . . . ?" she prompted.

"And . . . hurry up and answer me! I've asked you to marry me, Nerissa, and I can't live without you. What more do you want?"

After all the times Nerissa had discussed with Breck her various opinions on the matrimonial state, she didn't think he could have chosen a more ill-judged reply. She was instantly disappointed. In vain did she wait for Breck to speak those three little words she was longing to hear. Instead, he stood looking down at her, a playfully expectant expression upon his face, and his arms still wrapped protectively about her.

It would have been easy for her to accept his proposal

right then and there. She knew that he did, indeed, care for her, even if he hadn't said it in so many words. But of all the people of her acquaintance, she had thought Breck more than anyone would understand that she could never marry except for love.

"Is—is that all you have to tell me?" she asked, silently willing him to say the words she was longing to hear.

"Yes, and I'm waiting for an answer, Nerissa!"

"Could—could I give you my answer tomorrow?" she asked. Immediately she felt his arms stiffen about her.

She looked up at him then and saw that he was frowning slightly and there was a wariness to his expression.

"Tomorrow? Of course!" he said a little formally. "Although I am surprised. Why, Nerissa? Why can't you give me an answer now?"

She couldn't bring herself to look at him any longer, lest he see from her expression how deeply disappointed she was. "I think I should like to speak to my sister before I give my answer. I—I think it would be proper."

"You're right, of course!" said Breck, regaining a bit of his usual confidence. "And I suppose I should speak to Arthur Bridgewater. I'll call on him tomorrow. And then, my innocent, you may be assured there shall be no obstacles in our path and you and I will very soon be man and wife!"

Chapter 17

Nerissa was not immediately given an opportunity to speak to Anne about Breck's marriage proposal. Upon her return home from Pankhurst House she discovered that Anne had already retired to her room and that Arthur had left the house. Nerissa was disappointed.

She needed her sister's gentleness and kindness. Most of all, she needed her advice. Anne would know what to do: whether Nerissa should accept Breck's proposal even though he could not profess to love her. Anne would know whether Nerissa should cast aside all her plans and principles to marry a man who had missed every opportunity to confess his feelings.

Without Anne to guide her, Nerissa was sorely tempted to accept Breck, and hope that her love for him would be enough to carry them through.

She spent a rather sleepless night, during which she was haunted, first by her inability to make up her mind, and then by the memory of Breck's kiss. It would have been a very easy thing for Nerissa to convince herself that Breck did, indeed, care for her. Only a man in the deepest throes of love, she told herself, could kiss a woman so lovingly and evoke such a passionate response in return. She told herself most sensibly that he had to have proposed out of love. A man like Breck Davenant didn't issue marriage proposals lightly.

But in the end Nerissa doubted even that argument, and discounted such reasoning as nothing more than the wishful thinking of a silly romantic.

The following morning, as soon as she awoke, Nerissa threw a warm wrapper on over her nightclothes and padded down the hall to her sister's room. She rapped lightly at the door before opening it. Anne was awake, but still in bed, propped up by pillows against the massive oak headboard.

"Good morning!" said Nerissa. "And a merry Christmas Eve to you, Anne!"

Anne smiled back rather wanly. "And a happy Christmas Eve to you, Rissa dear."

Nerissa perched upon the bed and wondered how on earth she was going to tell her sister what had occurred the afternoon before. But one look into Anne's rather drawn expression, and the words died away on Nerissa's lips. "I asked after you last night, Anne, but Bellamy said you had already gone to bed. Are you feeling ill? May I get you anything?"

Anne shook her head slightly and turned a bit away. "I'm not ill, Rissa dear," she said in a tight little voice, "but I am sick—sick with heartache!"

"Dearest Anne, what has happened?" asked Nerissa in alarm. "What has distressed you so?"

Tears gathered in Anne's eyes and she said through tremulous lips, "Arthur—after you left last afternoon— we had the most horrid row!"

Nerissa clasped her sister's rather limp hand and held it fast. "But you and Arthur have always gotten along so vastly well. Anne, what on earth could you find to fight about?"

"You!" said Anne, sniffing mightily.

"Me? But what have I done?" She had a sudden thought. "Goodness, Arthur didn't find out about my going to the Westminster Pit, did he? Oh, he shall send me packing home, sure as check!"

"No, no! It wasn't that. It's all my fault—I brought it on myself," said Anne, her eyes filling again with unshed tears. "I mentioned Mr. Davenant's attentions toward you—an ill-judged remark, I see now! But how could I have known Arthur would react so?"

"Why? What did he do? What did you say?"

"I meant only to comment on how dashing he was. I mentioned that he and his cousin, Lord Crompton, could not have been finer gentlemen. Arthur became quite incensed! He said only a foolish female would admire a family made up of rascals and rogues."

"Goodness!" breathed Nerissa. "Just yesterday he was adjuring me to make up to the marquess!"

"That's not the worst of it! You see, I felt I had to defend Mr. Davenant and especially Lord Crompton—he's been so kind to me! So good! When I tried to tell Arthur of Lord Crompton's virtues, he became unreasonable. Why, I hardly recognized him! And then—oh, Rissa, he left in a very high dudgeon and I haven't seen him since!"

"Why, that sort of behavior doesn't sound at all like Arthur," said Nerissa, frowning.

Anne dashed away a tear with a delicate wave of her hand. "I was never more stunned! This last year of marriage to Arthur has been—well, not at all as I expected. Rissa dear, sometimes I think you are the cleverest and bravest girl alive, for *you* will not be forced into such a state as I find myself!"

"Oh, Anne, please don't cry," begged Nerissa consolingly. "Arthur shall come about—you'll see. And we shall all go on as we were before."

"Don't you see? That is exactly the problem! We cannot go on as before, for so much as changed! At last I have come to believe as you do—that no sacrifice is too small if it is made for love! If a woman truly and desperately loves a man, she is bound to show it by action and deed. *You* taught me that, Rissa!''

''Oh, Anne, I wish you wouldn't say such things,'' said Nerissa, feeling guilty indeed. ''My convictions are not always as strong as you think them to be.''

''But *you* would never marry where there is no love,'' said Anne with assurance. *''You* would never let your heart rule your head.''

But that was exactly what Nerissa had been prepared to do. Since the moment of Breck's proposal, she had been toying with the idea of accepting it, knowing full well that no mention of love had ever passed between them. She loved Breck and wished to be with him. She thought that if she married Breck, in time he would come to love her back. One look at her sister in the throes of romantic misery, and Nerissa realized she had been rainbow chasing.

Every last one of Nerissa's sisters had been caught in the same trap—marrying first and hoping that the love would come later. In Anne's tears, Nerissa was served proof on a platter that such hopes rarely came to pass. She was keenly disappointed but knew in her heart that Anne was right: it was wrong to marry where mutual love did not exist.

She remained with Anne for some time, trying to console her but feeling mightily depressed herself. When at last Nerissa left her, the time was well past noon and Anne was still in bed, still fighting tears, and still insisting that love was a most treacherous emotion.

Nerissa dressed, went downstairs, and encountered Bellamy on the landing. She asked after Arthur.

''I believe Lord Bridgewater is in, miss, but he has not yet left his room.''

''Would you tell him, please, when you see him that I'd like a word?''

''Of course, miss, but I wouldn't depend upon him for

some time yet. He had a rather late night of it, I might be forgiven to mention.''

The last time Arthur had had a late night, Nerissa reflected, he had been heartily ill the next day. If that episode were anything to judge by, she didn't think he would be presenting himself downstairs anytime soon.

At her writing table Nerissa put the last of the final touches to her manuscript so she would be ready to keep her appointment with the publisher. But every time she reread a page from her story, she found herself thinking of Breck. In a passage of dialogue she recognized bits of Breck Davenant's charmingly flippant style of address; in a scene of action she found herself dwelling upon Breck's graceful flair in movement. Over and over again, no matter what words presented on the page, she couldn't help but recall the wonder of his kiss.

Declining Breck's marriage proposal was going to be the hardest thing she had ever considered doing in her life. Breck had promised to call for her answer, and she knew he would not be pleased with what she had to say. Nerissa was feeling melancholy indeed when at last she turned over the final page of her manuscript and determined that it was at last finished and ready to be delivered.

In her room she had stored away a precious bit of new ribbon that she intended to use to tie up the sheaf of pages. She went upstairs to fetch it, along with her hat and gloves and warmest cloak. She rang for her maid and asked that the carriage be brought around, and she received in return a bit of a shock.

Mr. Breck Davenant, the maid informed her, had just that moment sounded the knocker and had been installed in the drawing room to await her appearance.

''Goodness, he's early!'' said Nerissa, heartily wishing she could postpone their meeting. ''Have the carriage brought around, as I said, and tell Bellamy to ask Mr. Davenant to wait—no, don't have him wait—I mean—oh, I must speak to Anne. Tell Mr. Davenant I shall be with him directly, but first I must speak with my sister!"

"But Lady Bridgewater is gone out, miss," said her maid.

Nerissa paused, one hand on the doorknob. "Out? Where did she go?"

"I couldn't say, miss, but Lady Bridgewater left some time ago. I think she did write down a message for you. Mr. Bellamy has it."

Nerissa dispatched the maid immediately with instructions to have the note brought straightaway and spent several anxious minutes pacing her bedroom. What could have caused Anne to leave the house without a word, she couldn't imagine. But every time Nerissa thought of Breck cooling his heels in the drawing room, she heartily wished her sister had stayed at home.

As soon as the maid reappeared with the note, Nerissa broke the wafer and read it. Its contents stunned her to such an extreme, she was forced to read it a second time.

Dear Rissa,

I have gone to meet Lord Crompton. What I do, I do for love. Please do not worry over me, and believe me when I say that Lord Crompton has been the kindest and most thoughtful of men. But you, dear sister, are more precious to me than anyone, for you have taught me that a woman must risk all for the man she loves. Please do not speak of what I have done, for I should not wish Arthur to learn of it. You shall hear from me shortly. I remain,

Your affectionate sister,
Anne

Nerissa's face had gone perfectly white when at last she looked up from reading the note for the third time. "How—how long ago—when did my sister leave?" she asked in a strangled voice.

"I'm sorry, miss, I couldn't say," replied the maid. "Mr. Bellamy might know, but he—"

"Have him attend me immediately!"

"Yes, miss, but I thought I saw him delivering a glass of wine down to your Mr. Davenant, but as soon as Mr. Bellamy is through—"

"Mr. Davenant!" Nerissa repeated in a rather frantic voice. "Of course! *He* will know what to do! Find Lord Bridgewater—ask him to come to the drawing room. And quickly! We haven't a moment to waste!"

Nerissa hurried down the stairs, her cloak flying loose behind her and the note crumpled in her hands along with her gloves and bonnet. In the hall outside the drawing room she took a moment to try to calm her skipping heart and hoped desperately that once Breck saw Anne's note, he would know exactly what was to be done.

But as Nerissa hesitated on one side of the drawing room door, Breck Davenant was on the other side, frowning over a very different piece of paper. While waiting for Nerissa to make an appearance, he had begun to idly travel the room and ended up at the small writing table on which was stacked, in neat order, the pages of her manuscript.

He smiled slightly and picked up the first page and read, with a rather unholy glee, the title of the piece: *The Count's Seduction.* Almost before he knew what he was about, he had read the first two pages of the manuscript and a rather unsettling realization began to take hold of him.

He had been half afraid the hero of such a gothic tale would prove to be a brooding, self-centered cad á la Byron. He was pleasantly surprised to discover otherwise. Nerissa, he discovered, was a skilled storyteller, but reading a bit farther down the page, he began to feel again a bit disquieted.

As he had expected, Nerissa had fashioned her hero to employ a few of his own mannerisms and behaviors. That did not disturb him. But he was disturbed when he realized the hero's physical description was unmistakably the same as his—the same color of the eyes and hair, the same build. More than disturbed, he found himself growing quite angry, for Nerissa had promised that if he agreed to serve as the model for her perfect hero, she would preserve his anonymity.

He could feel the heat of anger mantle his face. When the door opened and he saw Nerissa sweep into the room and immediately turn to shut the door herself, it was all he could do to keep from demanding to know what the devil she meant by such conduct.

"Nerissa!" he said in a voice that did little to hide his anger.

Then she turned and he saw her face. "Good God, what has happened?" he asked, immediately forgetting all about the stack of pages before him.

"It's Anne!"

"Is she injured? Is she ill?"

"She's—she's gone!" said Nerissa, her voice trembling. She thrust the note at him, saying, "I don't know when she left or how far a start she has had, but we must go after her! Please—*please* help me fetch her back! We haven't a moment to lose!"

Breck took her by the arm and gently led her over to a small settee drawn close by the fire. "Give me a moment to read this, but first I think you should sit down. Here, take a sip of this wine. You've gone ghostly pale."

"My feelings are of no import! Only please read the letter!"

He did then, and when he raised his eyes, he was looking very concerned and rather grim. "Has Bridgewater been told?"

"Been told what?" asked Arthur, entering the room. "Bellamy said I was needed in the drawing room. What's all the hubbub, Rissa?"

She responded by snatching the letter from between Breck's fingers and holding it out to Arthur. "I cannot bring myself to tell you—you must only read this." And when she thought he had been given a sufficient amount of time to master the contents of the note, she demanded in an agony of impatience, "Why do we stand about? Why do we not go after her?"

Arthur's face was flushed, and he had the look about him of a man mortally wounded. He raised his eyes to look first at Nerissa, then at Breck.

"Did—did you know of this beforehand?" he asked in a pained voice, holding the note as if it were about to catch fire.

"No, I didn't," said Breck. He took the letter back and quickly scanned it again. "I confess I didn't see it coming."

"But the other night, at the Hampden—we talked about this very thing! You said—"

"I'm sorry, Bridgewater," Breck replied in a simple but sincere voice.

"Arthur, it's not Breck's fault," said Nerissa, feeling the full weight of guilt upon her own shoulders. "If you must blame someone, you must blame *me! I* am the cause of this whole ghastly business, for it was I who put the notion in Anne's head!"

"You? You told Anne to run off with Crompton?" demanded Arthur, turning on her with fire in his eyes.

"No, but I told her about the plot for my book. I told her how the heroine sacrifices everything for the man she loves and how she and the hero elope to Gretna Green." Her voice caught on a sob, and she had to will herself not to cry. "Don't you see? It's all my fault! You have no one to curse but me and my silly notions and foolish romances. If only I had been more sensible, I might not have put such a wicked notion into her head."

Arthur's hands clenched into fists at his sides, and he held himself in rigid check for a moment. "Don't tease yourself, Rissa. I know you meant no harm," he said in a voice of hard-won calm. Then he turned and strode toward the door, saying, "Please excuse me."

"Arthur, wait! Where are you going?" cried Nerissa.

He paused at the door. "I'm going after my wife."

"I'll go with you," said Breck.

"No need. It's good of you to offer, but it might turn into a rather messy affair. I think it's best if I go alone and you stay with Nerissa."

"And miss a chance to see you draw my cousin's claret?" asked Breck, one brow raised questioningly.

Arthur stiffened. "Draw his claret? No such thing! I hope I may conduct myself at all times as a gentleman of breeding!"

Nerissa chimed in: "I'm going too, Arthur."

"Oh, no, you're not! You'll stay right here, young lady."

"Please, Arthur, I must go along! It's all my fault, and I must see that everything is put to rights!"

He remained unconvinced until Breck said, "We might need her—if for nothing else than to remove your wife from the scene while you deal with Crompton."

Arthur gave the matter a moment's thought. "A sensible notion. All right, you may come along, but you must do as you are told."

"I think it would be best if I rode ahead in my curricle," said Breck. He thrust the note into his vest pocket and drew on his gloves and greatcoat. "It's lighter and faster than your carriage, and I should be able to catch up to them sooner. If I find them, I shall detain them until you and Nerissa can follow along."

It sounded to Arthur like a suitable plan. Within a very few minutes Breck had departed in his curricle, leaving Nerissa and Arthur to follow behind in the barouche.

Their drive was a difficult one. The roads were slippery and rather treacherous and the going was slow and the atmosphere inside the carriage was tense and uncomfortable. Arthur sat rigidly upon the seat, schooling his gaze out the window, as unaware of the late afternoon dusk that gathered outside the coach as he was aware of Nerissa's presence inside.

Once the barouche was in motion, she tried again to

tell him how deeply sorry she was, but Arthur heard very little of what she said. His expression was grim, the lines about his mouth were very tight, and she thought he exuded an almost palpable anger that seemed to strengthen with each passing mile.

They rode for some time in uncomfortable silence. Arthur continued to stare rigidly out the window, and Nerissa did her best to keep from making frantic demands of the coachman to go faster by working her gloved fingers together into worried knots. She was vastly relieved when the carriage finally came to a halt.

They drew up before an inn situated not too far outside London. Breck's curricle was in the yard with Henry attending the horses. A very fine carriage bearing the Kendrew coat of arms had been drawn to one side and was partially hidden from view by a small wooden shed.

Breck was standing at the door to the inn when Nerissa and Arthur climbed down from the barouche. He motioned them inside, and when they were at last in the warmth of the hall, he said in a quiet voice, "They're here. Crompton has engaged a private parlor at the end of the hall, I understand, and they're in the room now."

"Why do we wait?" demanded Nerissa, feeling the frayed ends of her nerves about to catch fire. "We must intercede at once and save poor Anne!"

Breck rested a commanding hand upon her shoulder. "We must wait for your brother-in-law to decide what to do. Well, Bridgewater? What is it to be? Do we march upon the private parlor or do we get back in our carriages and return to London?"

Chapter 18

Arthur responded by turning on his heel and striding down the hall toward the back of the inn at a brisk and purposeful pace. Nerissa had to almost skip to keep up with him, and Breck followed close upon her heels with long, loose-legged strides.

At the end of the hall Arthur paused just a moment; then, with one quick movement, he opened the door and rushed into the room.

Nerissa was no more than a few steps behind him. As she hurried into the parlor, she had a quick impression of a small room with large, overstuffed chairs drawn toward the fire in a cozy grouping. Her attention, however, was immediately fixed upon the far side of the room, where Anne and Lord Crompton were seated at a table set against a window.

As the door flew open and the party of rescuers burst upon them, Lord Crompton jumped to his feet, sending his chair overturning and clattering to the floor.

"Bounder!" The word sprang from Arthur's lips. He stood glaring across the room, his fists clenched at his sides, and then he flew into action with astonishing speed. Before anyone could react, he dove forward to deliver a crashing blow to Lord Crompton's jaw that sent him sprawling.

Both Nerissa and Anne let out a shriek. Arthur ignored them both and advanced upon his victim. He stood over him, his face a mask of anger, his eyes gleaming with a look that was as frightening as it was uncommon for him.

Breck went after him to lay a restraining hand upon his shoulder. "Let the man get up, Bridgewater."

"I'll let him up!" promised Arthur. "And then I'll thrash the life from him!"

"Arthur, stop! Don't!" cried Nerissa, her hands covering her cheeks. Her outburst drew Arthur's attention for a moment, giving Lord Crompton an opportunity to scoot away toward the wall and out of Arthur's reach.

"Just what the devil was that for, Bridgewater?" demanded his lordship.

"That was for thinking you could seduce my wife out from under my very nose!" retorted Arthur.

"Seduce your wife? You're talking through your hat!"

"I'm no fool! I know perfectly well what you were doing here alone together!"

"Alone? You can hardly accuse Lady Bridgewater and me of being alone, when my mother has been with us the enter time!"

Arthur stopped short. "Your—your *mother?*" he repeated.

A female voice from one of the chairs by the fireplace interposed frigidly: "Yes! His *mother!*"

Everyone turned in astonishment. Lady Kendrew had risen from her chair by the fire and was looking upon Arthur with an expression of majestic wrath. "Be good enough to explain the meaning behind your actions, sir! How dare you launch an attack upon my poor son!"

"Aunt? What the devil are you doing here?" demanded Breck. "Or are you always privy to your son's elopements?"

"Elopement!" echoed Lady Kendrew scornfully. "Jamie is not eloping! Far from it! As if I would ever allow such a thing to occur!"

"But I don't understand!" said Nerissa. "You left a note for me, Anne, saying you were off with Lord Crompton— why, we all read it! Anne, you must explain what is happening!"

But Anne didn't heed her. She was, instead, looking at her husband with an expression of wonder upon her face. "Arthur, is this true? You thought I was eloping with Lord Crompton? Is that why you're here? To—to *save* me?" She went to him then, her eyes radiating the light of true happiness. She laid her gloved hand upon his sleeve and said in rapturous tones, "How heroic you were just now! How very, very dashing!"

Arthur's face flushed slightly. "Don't start that nonsense with me!" He possessed himself of both her hands and held them fast. "My actions had nothing whatever to do with being one of your cursed heroes! You might as well know that I—well, I suppose I should have told you so before, but you were always so damnably skittish and I didn't want to rush you and—and I love you, Anne!" he said very quickly before he could lose his nerve. His fingers tightened unconsciously about hers and he said a bit more tentatively, "Do you think, in time, you could come to love me too?"

"In time?" she repeated. "Dearest Arthur, don't you know? I love you already!

"You—you *do*? Anne, are—are you sure?"

She nodded vigorously. "I know I didn't feel that way when first we were married, but my feelings have altered and—and I *do* love you, Arthur! I have felt so for some time now!"

He relaxed visibly then, and let loose a deep breath of happy relief. "Dearest girl! Dearest, loveliest Anne!"

Lord Crompton thought it safe at last to get up from the floor and dust himself off. "Thank God that's settled!"

"But it's not settled," said Breck. "If you were not eloping with Lady Bridgewater, just what exactly were you doing here? Why the secret meeting, Crompton? And why were you always seen in close conversation with Lady Bridgewater?"

"Close conversation? Is that what you call it? More like pestering, I should say! Which is exactly what Lady Bridgewater was doing when we met the other night at the opera!"

"But why would Anne pester *you?*" asked Nerissa, clearly doubtful of his story.

"For this!" Lord Crompton picked up a piece of paper from the table and waved it aloft. "My father's pledge to support some wretched bill in the Lords. Lady Bridgewater has been after my mother and me to wear the old man down. It wasn't easy, but we prevailed upon him and here's his signature to prove it!"

"Since when," demanded Nerissa, "have you been interested in politics, Anne?"

"Since Mr. Davenant put the notion in my head. He said if I wanted to give Arthur the perfect Christmas gift, I must find out what he really wanted more than anything. I knew he wanted his Corn Bill passed, and I thought if Lord Kendrew would only support it, Arthur would have the votes he needed."

Arthur let loose her hands to wrap his arms about her. "Dearest, sweetest Anne! You did that for me?"

"I had no notion how you felt about me, you see," she said, smiling up at him with affection. "But I thought if I could give you such a gift, you might come to love me as I had grown to love you. It was Rissa's idea, really. She told me that if a woman truly loves a man, she must be willing to take great risks to show it." She cast a sly look toward her sister and added, "Now, if only she would act upon her own advice!"

Lady Kendrew let loose a noise that curiously resembled a harrumph. "I have had enough of these theatrical high jinks! Jamie, it is time we were returned to London. And, my dear Lady Bridgewater, if you are quite through with all this romantic nonsense, I hope you will recall your end of the bargain we have struck!"

"Bargain? What bargain, Anne?" asked Arthur.

"It is nothing you need concern yourself with," she said. "I merely promised Lord Crompton and Lady Kendrew that if they helped gain Lord Kendrew's support for your bill, in exchange I would arrange to have Mr. Davenant withdraw from the social scene this spring."

Breck smiled slightly, his interest piqued. "How, exactly, do you propose to do that?"

"Well, you can't very well reign as supreme bachelor in town if you are on your honeymoon trip, can you?"

"Be good enough, Lady Bridgewater, to allow me to make my own marriage proposals!" he said, but he didn't appear to be at all offended.

Lord Crompton was about to escort his mother from the room, but at this he turned, and with a keen interest asked, "Will you, then? *Will* you make her a proposal?"

"It may interest you to know, you impudent dog, that I have already asked the question of Miss Raleigh. If you will only be on your way, I may at last have my answer!"

"Then we shall leave at once! Anything to keep you from society's door for a Season!" Lord Crompton left then, taking his mother with him.

Nerissa knew the uncomfortable sensation of having every eye in the room trained upon her. She stood as if rooted to the floor, unable to move and quite unable to speak.

Anne came to her rescue, saying, "It is time we, too, were returned to London. Rissa dear, walk with me to the door." She linked her arm through Nerissa's and together they made their way down the hall toward the front door of the inn. "Is it true? Did Mr. Davenant ask you to marry him?" asked Anne in a lowered voice so neither Breck nor Arthur could overhear as they followed behind at a distance.

"Yes, he did, and I wanted to tell you about it last night and then again this morning. But all of this happened and—oh, Anne! I don't know what to think! Shall I accept him?"

"Why do you ask me? I can't advise you. You must follow only your heart."

"But what of *his* heart? I couldn't marry for love, knowing full well he could never love me back!"

Anne cast her an incredulous look. "Is that what you think?"

"I don't know what to think! I was never more confused in my life! I thought I knew all there was to know about love and men from reading novels, but I see now how ignorant I am! Only tell me what I am to do."

"You must decide for yourself, Rissa dear. But if you have learned anything tonight, you will have learned how happy Arthur and I have become. It is possible, I think, for two people to fall in love, given time."

They stepped out into the yard just as the coachman swung the barouche around and drew it up before the front door. Arthur moved forward to assist Anne into the carriage, and Nerissa would have followed, but was prevented doing so by Breck.

"Oh, no, you don't," he said, his firm grasp upon her arm. "You'll ride back to town with me."

"In your curricle? I'll freeze to death!"

"And it shall serve you right, after all the trouble you've caused."

"But Anne and Arthur—"

"Will thank me for it," he interrupted. "Don't you know you are sadly *de trop,* my dear? Give them some time together."

He led her over to his curricle, ignoring all her protests, and handed her up onto the seat in a rather ruthless manner. He climbed up after her and threw a fur rug across her legs. Then, taking up the reins, he said, "Stand away, Henry. You can ride back to town beside Bridgewater's coachman, I think."

Those words sent a trill of panic through her. Nerissa was afraid that if she were left alone with Breck, he might renew his proposal and press her for an answer. What, exactly, her answer was to be, she couldn't decide. The evening's events had left her confused and a little bewildered. No more was she sure of her own mind; no longer was she adamant that a marriage could not work where there was no love.

She cast about for an excuse to keep from having to travel with him. "Breck! We cannot ride back to town *alone!* What will people think?"

"They'll probably think I got tired of seeing you chasing after me on the streets and offered you a seat! Stand away, Henry!" he called, and with a slap of the reins on the horses' backs, they set off for London.

Chapter 19

They hadn't traveled many miles before Nerissa began to heartily wish Breck's favorite carriage wasn't a sporting curricle. In any other vehicle she might not have been in danger of freezing to death. But more important, in any other rig she might not have had to sit so close upon him.

She was acutely aware of his nearness as they sat on the narrow bench seat. The length of his long, muscled body was pressed against hers, and his arm brushed against her shoulder every time he was obliged to adjust his hold upon the reins.

It was, she thought, a rather sweet torture to have to sit beside him so, knowing how much she loved him and was attracted to him, and knowing full well he did not at all appear to reciprocate those feelings. She drew the fur rug higher up under her chin to stave off the cold and to try to build a bit of a barrier between her and Breck. It didn't work. She remained burningly aware of his every masculine movement throughout their drive back to the city.

Once they left the inn yard, neither Breck nor Nerissa spoke. She was glad of it, for she rather suspected that if he were to take advantage of their situation to try to make love to her or press her for an answer to his suit, her only response would be to burst into tears.

She could not recall a time when she had ever felt so confused or quite so emotional. She could only hope that when at last he did demand an answer from her, he would give her some hint of his feelings for her. In the meantime, he concentrated only on tooling his horses, and Nerissa was able to relax her guard a bit.

But when the dirt of the country road was left behind them and they began traveling over familiar London cobbles, she felt a bit of panic rise again.

"This is not the way to my sister's house," she said, and looked up at him to see a most determined expression on his face.

"No, but it is the way to my brother's house," he replied.

"But I—I don't want to go there!"

"My dear, you have no choice. We have some unfinished business between us, I think."

He drew up in Grosvenor Square and leapt gracefully down to the pavement. "Will you come inside, Nerissa?"

Almost, she refused, but he stood looking up at her so expectantly, his strong hand extended up to her, she had no choice but to lay her hand in his and allow him to help her down.

He led her up the steps of the house. The large front door opened magically at their approach and a beam of light from inside the front hall lit their way in the early evening darkness. Lord Pankhurst's butler bowed them in, and two very smart, liveried footmen appeared from the netherworlds of the great house to relieve Breck of his coat and gloves.

"Is my brother in?" he asked.

"I regret he is not," said the butler. "Lord and Lady Pankhurst and the children have gone out. I do not suppose, however, they shall make a late night of it, it being

Christmas Eve and all. If you'd care to, sir, you shall find a fire already made up in the family saloon."

With a solicitous hand at her elbow, Breck led Nerissa into a small, cozy room that was decorated comfortably but still managed to maintain the first style of elegance. In a polished brass grate, a small but inviting fire burned brightly, and Nerissa made for it immediately. She was still battling an urge to let her teeth chatter after such a cold drive, but she was also hoping that the warmth of the flames would help calm her skipping nerves.

The footman softly pulled the door closed, leaving them quite alone together. Breck eyed her speculatively. "You might want to sit down," he said, pulling a chair forward. "This may take a while."

The moment she had been dreading had come at last! She clasped her hands together in a very tight grip and turned to face him. There was a light in his eyes, a rather dangerous glow she had never seen before, and it put her on her guard.

"I—I think I should prefer to stand," she said in a breathless voice that did not at all sound like her own.

He joined her by the fire. "At least lay off your things, Nerissa, and warm yourself before you catch your death."

"I'm quite comfortable," she said falsely bright, but when she saw that he was watching her again with a rather peculiar look to his eye, she thought she might have sounded a bit ungrateful. "Well, I suppose it would be a good idea to take my cloak off, at least."

"As you wish." He took the cloak from her and spread it over the back of the chair. When he had finished that task and turned back to face her, he saw that she had decided to remove her gloves and bonnet after all.

Breck took a cigarillo from his pocket and lit it. He drew deeply against it as he watched her nervously arrange, with the utmost care and attention, those items on a nearby table.

"Nerissa," he said once he thought she had made

enough of a show of smoothing imaginary wrinkles from her kid gloves, "I am about to make a rather uncompromising demand upon you."

"A—a demand?" she repeated, thinking that these were hardly the words of a man in love about to renew his suit.

"Yes. You see, I've read your book. Not all of it, but enough to know—"

"Good gracious! My *book!*" she exclaimed. Her hands flew up to cover her cheeks. "Merciful heavens, I forgot all about it! I had an appointment to meet Mr. Heble, and in all the hubbub—oh, what must he think?" In an instant she was moving about the room, gathering up the very same bonnet, gloves, and cloak she had just finished discarding.

"It doesn't matter now what he thinks," said Breck. "I cannot allow the book to be published."

Nerissa was in the process of setting her bonnet back on her head and tying its ribbons into a rather lopsided bow beneath her chin. At Breck's words she stopped and turned to look at him with surprise.

"Cannot allow—? What do you mean?"

"I mean there is no need for you to rush off to your Mr. Heble with your manuscript tucked under your arm. I intend to see to it that the book never gets published, Nerissa."

It took her a moment or two to assimilate his words. "But why? You know it has ever been my plan to sell my book and earn my living as a writer. You know I have no choice but to do so if I'm not to be married!"

"Is that still your plan, Nerissa?" he asked. "Do you still intend never to marry?"

Now or never was the time for Breck to give her some indication of his feelings. Instead, he stood looking at her with an unblinking gaze. Perhaps he needed some encouragement? She said, "That has always been my plan, but like many things in life—as I have learned—plans may be changed."

"Nerissa," he said, advancing slowly upon her, "I asked

you to marry me yesterday. I'm still awaiting your answer. What is it to be?"

There was something a little unnerving in the way he was looking at her. "I—I've given the matter a great deal of thought and—and are you truly certain you wish to marry me?" she asked, offering him yet another chance to declare his feelings.

"Yes, I'm truly certain." He continued to close in upon her.

She swallowed hard and tried to find her voice but found instead that she had backed up against a table, prohibiting any further retreat.

He tossed his cigarillo into the grate and eliminated the last of the distance between them. He stood so close that she could smell the rich aroma of tobacco on his clothes and could feel his breath set the curls on the top of her head to dancing. Almost before she realized what he was about, his hands had worked to untie the ribbons beneath her chin and magically disposed of her bonnet. He levered a finger against the smooth white of her throat and tilted her head back so she had no choice but to look up at him.

"Say yes, Nerissa," he commanded in a quiet voice. "Say you shall marry me."

If only he wouldn't press her so. If only he would remove his fingers from beneath her chin so she didn't have to look him in the eye when she refused him, for refuse him she would.

Despite Anne's advice, despite the temptation of her own heart, Nerissa knew she could never marry a man who didn't love her. She had witnessed too many lessons from her sisters and their disastrous marriages to believe she could find happiness with a man who didn't return her love. Oh, Anne and Arthur had married without love and had come to care for each other over time, but it had taken them almost a year to realize their feelings for one another.

Perhaps, over time, Breck, too, would come to love her.

But what if, like Anne, Nerissa had to wait a year for him to love her back? What if she had to wait *two* years?

She had a sudden vision of herself, married to Breck, and waiting month after month, year after dreary year, for him to toss her a kind or tender word. No, she decided with resolution, she could not live that way. She would rather suffer the hurt of not having Breck at all than to bear the heartache of knowing he could not return her regard.

He stood looking down at her with such expectancy that she was hard pressed to form her answer into words. That telltale warmth she had noticed before in his eyes was still there, and he was studying her with an unnerving intensity.

She closed her eyes against him and said, "Breck, I know you think that we should suit, but—"

"Open your eyes, Nerissa."

She did, but still she could not bring herself to look at him, and settled her gaze instead on the folds of his cravat.

Determined, he tilted her head a little farther back until she had no choice but to look at him. He had often thought that her eyes were a mirror to her every thought, and at that very moment he could see in them a hesitancy and doubt. He was a little stunned to think she was actually considering rejecting him, and said cautiously, "Nerissa, do you suspect the sincerity of my proposal? You needn't! I very much want you to marry me. In fact, I'm relying upon your doing just so."

That gave her some hope. "Why? *Why* do you want me to marry you?"

He smiled slightly. "Because I have found I cannot live without you. Besides, everyone who knows us expects it."

Her spirits collapsed. She had given him every opportunity to say those three precious words, and still he had not. She was disappointed and desperately hurt. There was nothing to do now but politely decline his proposal and beg to be returned to her sister's house.

She tried to look him in the eye, but couldn't. She had

to focus again on the folds of his cravat as she said quickly, before her resolve failed, "I am very mindful of the honor you have done me and very grateful to have been singled out to receive your attention, but I must decline your very flattering offer."

"You're refusing me?" he asked, astonished. "Nerissa! Why?"

She didn't want to have to explain why. She wanted only to go home to her own bed and have a good cry. "There— there are any number of reasons—"

"Name one!" he demanded harshly. "Tell me one good reason you won't marry me!"

"Breck, I cannot marry where there is no love!" She had blurted out the words before she could stop them, and when she looked quickly up at him, she saw that he was standing stock-still, his expression unreadable.

He didn't respond for several moments. Then he said in an even, emotionless tone, "I see." He loosened his hold of her and took a step back as some impulse forced him to place some distance between them.

"Are—are you angry with me?"

"Angry? No. A little stunned, perhaps, but not angry." He studied her face for a moment, then said cautiously, "Nerissa, did it never occur to you that love may come in time? You may not love me now, but did you never think my love for you just might be enough for both us?"

For a moment she could hardly credit she had heard right. "Your—your love for *me?*"

"Yes, Nerissa. I love you. And I think I can make you happy, if only you'll give me the chance."

She thought her heart would swell to twice its normal size. "Oh, Breck! I'm *already* happy!" she cried, and promptly threw her arms about his neck.

He gave a short laugh of surprise, then clasped her shoulders and put her gently but firmly away. "Nerissa! What the—If you aren't the most unpredictable—"

"Yes! Oh, yes, Breck, I *will* marry you! I didn't want to

refuse you the first time, but I was afraid that if I married you, I'd end up just like my sisters. You never said you loved me, you see."

"Do you mean to tell me that after all the romances you have read and all the romantic fiction you have scribbled, you still don't know how to tell when a man is in love with a woman?"

She gave her head a small shake. "I'm hoping you shall teach me."

He took a step closer and framed her face between his large, tanned hands. "With pleasure," he murmured, and he lowered his mouth to hers.

His kiss was gentle and warm and wonderful. Nerissa merely stood, savoring the feel of his lips on hers, marveling over how perfect it felt to be standing within his tender thrall.

After a moment, the tenor of their embrace changed. Breck possessively wrapped his arms about her, and his kiss deepened and became more demanding. That little spark of electricity once again sprang to life within her, and Nerissa pressed herself against him, kissing him back with a fervor that matched his own.

Sometime later, having kissed his bride-to-be into a weak and very pliant young woman, Breck raised his head. "You *are* an innocent. And I think I shall take great pleasure in changing that."

"I cannot say there is anything about you that I would change," she replied through a very happy fog. "To me, you shall always be the perfect hero."

"And I shall gladly be so as long as you and I are the only ones who know of it," he replied, very much amused.

"Oh, I want everyone to know how perfectly wonderful you are—and so they shall as soon as my book is published."

That sent a small frown across his brow. "Do you mean to tell me you still intend to be an authoress, even after we are married?"

"Why, yes. Breck, please don't ask me to stop writing my stories."

"I won't, if that's your heart's desire. But you must leave me out of the business, and you must start by changing the book you've already written."

"What's wrong with my book? I thought to have captured very well your most herolike qualities."

"That's just the problem, my dear—you've captured me *too* well! Everyone who reads your book shall recognize me in your cursed Count du Laney! I won't have it, Nerissa. And you gave me a solemn promise you would preserve my identity if I agreed to pose as the model for your story."

She was a little doubtful. "But, Breck, I *can't* change my book now! Besides, in my story Count du Laney isn't at all like you. He is proud and haughty—"

"As am I!"

"And he takes great delight in holding others up to ridicule and setting one family member against another!"

"A criticism that has often been hurled in my direction. Apply to my aunt Kendrew if you have any doubts."

She gave the matter a moment's thought. "I could change the hero a bit, I suppose, but I'm not sure that I would know how."

"Make him something of a romantic—soften his edges a bit!"

"I think I shall need some help to do so," she said, looking up at him with a rather impish light to her eyes. "I shall need a model if I am to create a perfect hero who is also tender and a bit of a romantic. I dare say I could stand at the corner of St. James's Street and examine all the men passing by to see if any of them measures up to such a hero."

Breck tightened his hold about her in a rather possessive way and said determinedly, "You shall do nothing of the sort, young lady!"

He might have hurled some other loving threats in her direction had not a footman, at that very moment, flung open the door to the saloon to admit Lord and Lady Pankhurst and the three eldest of their children.

Lady Pankhurst was the first to enter the room, and stopped short upon seeing her brother-in-law locked in a most intimate embrace with the young lady he had professed to love just days before.

Happy as she was to have come upon such a scene, Lady Pankhurst still let out a short gasp of surprise that captured the lovers' attention.

"Why, what is this? Breck, have you—? Has she—?"

"Yes and yes! Now, be good enough to leave us, Jane!" he said ruthlessly. "Simon, if you are at all interested in seeing me leg-shackled at last, you shall take your family away now!"

"With pleasure," said the marquess with a benevolent smile. He began to shepherd his wife and children out of the room. "And once you are done taming that rascal of a brother of mine, Miss Raleigh, you must come to us in the drawing room. Just a family gathering, of course. A Christmas Eve in front of the Yule log, roasting pears, and wishing one another happy."

"And if Breck refuses to join us, you must come to us on your own, Miss Raleigh," said Jane, feeling her husband tow her relentlessly toward the door. "After all, you are part of the family now!"

"Don't keep us waiting too long," adjured the marquess just as the door closed upon him.

"Families!" said Breck with loathing when they were once again alone. He tightened his hold about Nerissa and crushed her against him. "Now, where was I?"

"You were about to help me find a model for my hero," said Nerissa helpfully.

"Rot! I was about to kiss you until your pretty little head spins."

"But, Breck, I must have help if I am to rewrite my book!"

"My dear young woman, if you wish to write about love, you have only to observe me!" he said.

And then, knowing full well that he would take the greatest pleasure in serving as the model for all her future research needs, he tilted her head back and kissed her soundly until all thoughts of heroes and manuscripts were long forgotten.

ABOUT THE AUTHOR

Nancy Lawrence lives with her family in Aurora, Colorado. She is the author of two Zebra Regency romances: *Delightful Deception* and *A Scandalous Season*. Nancy loves hearing from her readers, and you may write to her c/o Zebra Books. Please include a self-addressed stamped envelope if you wish a response.

WATCH FOR THESE ZEBRA REGENCIES